SCREAM STREET

Book Seven

INVASION OF THE NORMALS

D0968225

The fiendish fun continues at
www.screamstreet.com

SCREAM STREET

Book Seven
INVASION OF THE NORMALS

TOMMY DONBAVAND

CANDLEWICK PRESS

Text copyright © 2009 by Tommy Donbavand
Illustrations copyright © 2009 by Cartoon Saloon Ltd.

First U.S. edition 2012

Library of Congress Cataloging-in-Publication Data is available.

Library of Congress Catalog Card Number pending

ISBN 978-0-7636-5759-8

12 13 14 15 16 17 18 QGB 10 9 8 7 6 5 4 3 2 1

Printed in Burlington, WI, U.S.A.

This book was typeset in Bembo Educational.
The illustrations were done in ink.

Candlewick Press
99 Dover Street
Somerville, Massachusetts 02144

visit us at www.candlewick.com

For my brother, Bryan –
Sorry for accidentally punching you in
the face on Christmas morning, 1980,
when you were two years old

Meet the residents

Luke Watson

Cleo Farr

Resus Negative

Dixon

Sir Otto Sneer

Samuel Skipstone

Alston and Bella
Negative

Eefa Everwell

Doug

Dr. Skully

Niles Farr

Mr. and Mrs. Watson

Who lives where

A Sneer Hall

B Central Square

C Everwell's Emporium

D No. 2: The Crudleys

E No. 5: The Movers

F No. 11: Twinkle

G No. 13: Luke Watson

H No. 14: Resus Negative

I No. 21: Eefa Everwell

J No. 22: Cleo Farr

K No. 26: The Headless Horseman

L No. 27: Femur Ribs

M No. 28: Doug, Turf, and Berry

N No. 32: Simon Howl

O No. 39: The Skullys

Previously on Scream Street...

When Luke Watson first transformed into a werewolf, his parents were able to lock him in his bedroom and keep themselves safe. However, when Luke tried to defend a fellow student from the school bully, there was no one to stop his inner wolf from bursting out and fighting back.

The bully, Steven Black, escaped unharmed. But as a result of the attack, Luke and his parents were moved to Scream Street: a secure location for unusual life-forms in a world parallel to their own. His parents were terrified, so Luke teamed up with wannabe vampire Resus Negative and Cleo Farr, an Egyptian mummy, and set out on a quest to find six relics left behind by the founding fathers of Scream Street. Once the relics were gathered, Luke was able to open a magical doorway back home—but seeing how happy he had become among his new friends, his parents decided to stay on in Scream Street.

The doorway, however, not having been used for its intended purpose, remained open and was soon discovered by Steven Black. The bully took a deep breath and stepped through. . . .

Chapter One
The Games

Eerie organ music sounded as the vampire skidded around the corner, a giant mummy lumbering after him. The vampire glanced over his shoulder and bared his fangs at his bandaged pursuer but nonetheless picked up the pace.

A gangly banshee appeared behind the mummy, her wild, knotted hair flapping as she ran. "YOU CAN'T STOP ME!" she screeched, momentarily blocking out the mysterious chords with her piercing voice.

After the banshee came a skeleton, closely followed by a zombie, lurching slowly but steadily at the back of the pack. The creepy music grew louder . . . and louder . . .

And then stopped.

Everyone dived for the nearest chair. The mummy and the banshee grabbed the first two, while the skeleton and the vampire were forced to race around the perimeter an extra time before they could sit down.

Finally, the zombie staggered to a halt.

"You're out, Turf!" called Luke Watson, pulling one of the chairs away to the side of the room. "OK, Mr. Howl—more music, please!"

The ghost of Mr. Howl gave a thumbs-up, then turned back to the translucent church organ and resumed playing. Turf the zombie limped off to the food table, hoping he hadn't missed the deep-fried spleens. He hadn't.

"Great party!" said Cleo Farr.

"Your dad certainly seems to be enjoying himself," Luke said with a grin, indicating the huge mummy once again racing around the small circle of chairs.

"He's just happy that you decided to stay in Scream Street," said Cleo, squeezing Luke's arm. "We all are."

Luke smiled at her, then turned at the sound of laughter on the other side of the room. His mom was trying on the cape that belonged to their vampire neighbor Bella Negative and sticking out her teeth like fangs.

The beautiful witch standing with them, Eefa Everwell, raised a perfectly manicured finger, purple sparks fizzing around the long, elegant nail. "I could give you some real fangs if you like."

Mrs. Watson held up her hands in mock terror. "It's enough excitement just living next door to vampires, thank you very much!"

Steven Black watched this nightmare through the crack between the doors of the cupboard in which he was hiding. There were monsters out there — and they were playing party games!

Since he had stepped through the doorway

into Scream Street earlier that day, he'd wandered around, exploring the strange neighborhood. The houses were weird—all tall and twisted, with black slate roofs and wooden window shutters. It was like being on the set of a spooky, old-fashioned horror movie.

Curious to see inside one of the houses, Steven had climbed in through an open window. When he heard people coming, he hid in a cupboard.

He must have fallen asleep, because when he woke up, he was still in the cupboard, his back stiff. He had been about to open the door and climb out when the organ music had started.

"Who'd have thought it?" said a voice.

Luke jumped. His friend Resus Negative had crept up behind him. "Don't do that!"

Resus grinned. "I mean it, though — who would have thought we'd see your mom and dad hanging out with everyone like this?"

The music came to a sudden stop, and Dr. Skully, Scream Street's skeletal teacher, found himself without a chair. "Sorry," called Luke as he slid another seat away and signaled for Mr. Howl to resume playing.

"Speaking of which," said Resus, scanning the room, "where *is* your dad?"

"In the backyard," replied Luke, "playing pin the tail on the dragon."

"This I *have* to see!" The young vampire cried. "You coming?"

"After this game's finished," said Luke. "And after I've found something to drink. I had one of Cleo's lotus-flower fritters earlier, and I'm dying of thirst."

"There's nothing wrong with my fritters!" cried Cleo. "But I have got some lemonade if you want some."

"Thanks!" Luke took the bottle from her and pulled hard at the cork. He grunted in frustration when it wouldn't budge.

"Let me try," said Resus, snatching it from his friend. The vampire sank one of his glistening fangs into the top.

Luke grinned. "Watch out, bottle—he's going to bite your neck!"

"Ha, ha," retorted Resus, twisting around in an effort to dislodge the cork. Drool began to drip from his fangs and run down the sides of the bottle.

"Eww!" exclaimed Cleo. "I'm not drinking that." She pulled her bandages up to cover her mouth in disgust.

The room fell silent as Simon Howl stopped playing once again. Cleo's dad slumped into a chair next to the banshee.

"Mr. Negative is out!" announced Luke. As the music started up for the last time, the two finalists circled the remaining seat.

A *pop!* signaled that the lemonade was open. Luke grabbed a glass and turned back to Resus. "Fill me up—" he began, then bit his lip to stop himself from laughing. The top was still firmly on the bottle; it was Resus's false fangs that had popped free.

"Don't shay a shingle word," said Resus, slobbering. He grasped the fake fangs like a corkscrew and finally freed the top. Born a normal child to vampire parents, he wore the fake fangs and dyed his hair jet black to avoid looking out of place in his family.

"My lips are sealed." Luke grinned as Resus filled his glass. "In fact, if you stick a cork on the other tooth as well, you've got yourself a set of safety fangs. You'll never bite your tongue again!"

With a final dramatic chord, Simon Howl's organ recital came to an end, and the mummy squeezed his giant frame into the single chair.

"Mr. Farr is the winner!" Luke announced to much applause.

"CONGRATULATIONS!" bellowed the banshee.

Luke's dad appeared in the doorway. "Now that we've finished musical chairs," he said, "I've got an idea for a new game—musical scares!"

The other residents gathered around him to hear the rules.

"As Scream Street's honorary normals," began Mr. Watson, "it took Susan and me a long time to get used to some of you."

"You can say that again," Alston Negative said with a grin. "I lost count of the number of times you fainted when you saw me!" A ripple of laughter spread across the room, and Luke's mom joined her husband.

"OK, OK," said Mr. Watson, smiling. "So, let's test how our nerves are holding up. I want each of you in turn to do your best to scare us! Simon—if you'd be so kind as to set the scene. . . ."

The party guests began to chatter excitedly as Simon Howl shimmered into view at his organ to play another dirge.

Turf the zombie lurched toward Mr. and Mrs. Watson, his arms stretched out in front of him. "Brains! Brains!"

Luke's dad shook his head. "You'll have to do better than that, Turf!"

Mrs. Watson laughed. "Who's next?"

Eefa Everwell stepped up to try out a little magic on them.

Resus turned to Luke. "You could win this easily!"

"How?"

"Duh!" said Resus, tapping Luke on the head. "You're a werewolf, remember."

"I don't think that's a good idea," said Cleo.

"Cleo's right," agreed Luke. "It was my wolf that brought my mom and dad here in the first place. They were terrified every time I transformed."

Resus rolled his eyes. "And the point of the game is . . . ?"

Luke still wasn't convinced. "If I transform in a room full of people, I could really hurt someone," he said.

"OK," said Resus. "Just change your head or something. I thought you were able to control which part of your body transforms."

"I am," Luke replied defensively.

"Well, now's your chance to prove it! Unless

 9

you're too afraid to accept the challenge, of course. . . ."

"Too afraid?" scoffed Luke. "No way! I'm just waiting for you to think up something worth betting for."

"Don't worry about that," Resus replied. "If you win, you can have my entire collection of medieval weapons. But if I win . . ." He reached inside his cloak and pulled out a small golden casket decorated with hieroglyphics.

Luke opened the box to reveal a vial of witch's blood, a werewolf's claw, a skull, a vampire's fang, a mummy's heart, and a diseased zombie's tongue. "You want to try to win the relics from me?" he asked.

"Not all of them," said his friend. "Just the vampire's fang. Count Negatov was my ancestor, after all."

"I don't know . . ." began Luke. He had gone through a lot to find the founding fathers' gifts, and the thought of giving them up felt strange.

"Oh, come on," encouraged Resus. "It's not like you need them now that you've decided to stay on in Scream Street. I thought they'd make

cool souvenirs to remind us of everything we went through to get them."

"I like the sound of that," said Cleo. "There are just enough for two each. I'd like to have the mummy's heart and the skull—if that's OK."

"All right, then," agreed Luke, shaking off the strange feeling. "I never would have found them if it wasn't for you guys, and I'm glad they're going to good homes."

"In that case," said Resus, peering into the casket, "I'll have the bottle of witch's blood to go with my vampire fang . . ."

"Leaving me with the zombie's tongue and the werewolf's claw," finished Luke. "That was easy enough!"

On the other side of the room, Resus's dad was downing a pint of blood to try to spook Luke's parents.

Mrs. Watson shook her head. "Like plasma off a bat's back, Alston!"

Resus nudged Luke. "But don't think it gets you out of transforming that ugly mug of yours," he said. "You've still got to try to scare your mom and dad and win my weapons—if that's OK with Little Miss Sensible, of course."

"Oh, why not?" said Cleo with a laugh. "I don't suppose it'll hurt if you only do it for a minute or two."

Luke closed his eyes and focused. When he had first started transforming, it had happened when he'd been really angry. All that stuff about werewolves appearing only when there was a full moon was just in the movies; the change was actually triggered when the rage inside could no longer be contained and burst out in animal form.

Over time, Luke had found that he could set off his transformations simply by thinking about something that made him angry—and, even better, he could focus that fury and push it toward particular areas of his body.

This was what he would do now, even if it was merely a party trick this time. He thought back to the moment when hordes of the faceless men known as Movers had invaded his home and brought him and his family to Scream Street. Even though he was now happy here, the fact that he and his parents had had no choice in the matter still made him furious.

The anger bubbled inside him like a witch's steaming cauldron, and Luke concentrated on

channeling it to change the shape of his face. His nose stretched out to form a snout, complete with long whiskers. Jagged teeth burst from his gums, and his tongue grew thicker and wider. Last, rough fur sprouted across his face, and his ears rose up to sit high on the top of his head.

The transformation complete, Luke leaped in front of his parents, threw back his head, and howled. Before either of them could react, a scream rang out from behind them—the scream of a child.

"STAY AWAY FROM ME!"

Chapter Two
The Doorway

The voice made Luke jump, not only because he hadn't been expecting it but also because it sounded vaguely familiar. The cupboard behind his parents burst open, and a boy jumped out, trembling with fear.

"It's you!" he yelled, pointing at Luke. "You're back to get me!"

Luke's throat contracted, and a flicker of recognition flashed through his mind. It *couldn't* be . . . He stepped forward.

The boy leaped away from him, crashing straight into Alston Negative, who spilled his drink.

"Hey!" exclaimed the vampire, his fangs bared as he glared down at the stain on his shirt. "Careful!"

The boy pushed the vampire aside and ran for the door, colliding with Dr. Skully as he did so. Simon Howl materialized beside the skeleton. "Are you OK, son?" he asked the trembling boy.

He was sobbing now, tears of pure terror streaming down his cheeks. He forced his way past Dr. Skully and raced down the hallway toward the front door. Luke, Resus, and Cleo gave chase.

"Wait!" Luke called, but the boy didn't stop.

Instead, he dashed out of the house and across the front lawn, not daring to look back. He was halfway across the yard when a green decomposed hand burst out of the grass and grabbed hold of his ankle. To the boy's horror, the hole widened and another of Scream Street's resident zombies

clambered out, his face covered in weeping sores, insects crawling through his matted hair.

"Dude," grinned Doug. "I hear there's a party going on!"

With a final strangled yelp, the boy collapsed to the grass in a dead faint.

"Is that who I think it is?" asked Mrs. Watson, staring down at the unconscious boy on the front lawn.

"It's Steven Black," confirmed Luke. "I used to go to school with him—before we came to Scream Street."

"Hang on," said Alston. *"Before* you came to Scream Street? You mean . . . he's from *your* world?" A murmur of unease rippled through the small crowd of residents.

Luke nodded. "He's the bully my werewolf went for. The one that brought me to the attention of G.H.O.U.L."

"Then it's hardly surprising that he reacted the way he did when he saw you transform," said Eefa Everwell, kneeling beside the boy. "I think he's just in shock."

"You're missing the point," cried Alston.

"There's a *normal* here in Scream Street—a normal from another world! Who cares what's wrong with him?"

"*I* care," Mrs. Watson responded. "He's just a child."

"Yes," called a voice from the back of the group. "A *normal* child!"

Luke felt his cheeks redden. He'd known nothing good would come from accepting Resus's bet.

"Let's all try to calm down," said Bella Negative. "He's here now, and there's no point arguing about it. We need to work out what he's doing in Scream Street."

"Maybe he's been brought here by the Movers," suggested Cleo. "G.H.O.U.L. might have arranged it."

"The dude doesn't look like one of us," said Doug.

"Neither does Luke," Mr. Watson pointed out, "but *he* belongs here."

"Doug's right, Dad," said Luke. "Steven Black might be a lot of things, but he's not a werewolf or anything like that. He's a normal."

"Then how did the boy get here?" demanded Simon Howl.

"You don't suppose . . . ?" began Resus. "You don't suppose the doorway to your world is still open, do you?"

Luke thought back to the moment he had finally assembled the six founding fathers' relics in Scream Street's central square, just a few hours ago. A doorway of shimmering, multicolored light had sprung into being, through which he had been able to see the outside of his old house, on his old street. "I don't see how it could be," he said thoughtfully. "We brought the relics back here with us."

"Maybe," said Cleo, "but did you actually *see* the doorway close?" When Luke didn't reply, the mummy turned to the others who had been there. "Did anyone?" They all shook their heads.

"We'd better go and check it out," said Resus.

Cleo's dad, Niles Farr, bent to pick up the still unconscious bully. "And return the boy to his own world," he added.

Luke, Resus, and Cleo led the way to Scream Street's central square. There, still glimmering softly, was the doorway of light.

"Dude!" breathed Doug. "It's like our very own rainbow, man!"

"Not quite," Mr. Watson interjected. "There are only six colors: red, blue, yellow, purple, green, and orange. If this was a real rainbow, the purple would be split into indigo and violet to make seven."

Mrs. Watson nudged her husband in the ribs. "I love it when you get technical," she teased.

Niles Farr, still holding the boy, took a step toward the doorway.

"Hang on, Dad," said Cleo. "You can't just dump him on the sidewalk. He needs to be taken home."

"I do not know where he lives," admitted the huge mummy.

"I do," said Luke's mom. "I'll go with you."

Resus raised his eyebrows. "No offense, Mr. Farr, but I've been to Luke's world. You'll stick out like a fang on a frog!"

Mr. Watson stepped forward. "I'll carry him, then."

Luke grabbed his arm. "You can't!" he insisted. "What if the doorway closes and you both get stuck on the other side without me?"

Cleo shivered at the thought. She and Resus had gone through the doorway when it first

 19

opened, to get a brief glimpse of Luke's world, and had become trapped there for a while. It had been a terrifying experience.

Luke's dad gazed around at the vampires, zombies, skeletons, and ghosts who made up the rest of the group. "Well, unless we want to scare our old neighbors silly, I can't really see another option."

"*I* shall carry the boy," announced a deep voice. Striding across the square was a tall man with thick, dark hair. He wore black mirrored sunglasses, and a long leather coat flapped in his wake.

"Mr. Chillchase!" exclaimed Luke. Zeal Chillchase was a Tracker for G.H.O.U.L.—a shapeshifter who hunted out unusual life-forms and arranged for their relocation to places like Scream Street. He had arrested Luke, Resus, and Cleo during their visit to Luke's world, and the trio still felt a little nervous in his presence.

"I didn't know he was still here," grumbled Resus under his breath.

"There was much to be discussed with your landlord," said Zeal, giving the young vampire a steely look. He took the unconscious boy from

Niles and turned to Luke's mom. "You know where the boy lives?"

"Yes, it's not too far," replied Mrs. Watson. "Half an hour's walk at most. I had to go there once to get Luke's soccer cleats back."

Luke's cheeks reddened as he recalled the incident.

"Then we should leave now," announced the

 21

Tracker sharply, and without another word, he carried the slumbering bully through the doorway and out of Scream Street.

Mrs. Watson took a deep breath. "We're leaving now, apparently." She smiled briefly at her husband and followed Zeal through the shimmering portal.

"Well, at least *that* problem's solved," said Alston.

"Let's get back to the party," suggested Mr. Watson. "It's my turn on the bucking banshee!"

"Don't you think we'd better wait here, just in case?" Luke asked.

"In case of what?" Simon Howl asked. "In case the boy overpowers G.H.O.U.L.'s leading Tracker and makes his way back here?" The other adults laughed.

"It'll be fine," said Mr. Watson, ruffling his son's hair. "But stay here if it makes you feel better." Talking among themselves, he and the others wandered back to the party.

"How come the doorway stayed open even though we took the relics away?" said Resus once the three friends were on their own.

"I have no idea," replied Luke. "But I know

someone who might be able to help us." He pulled a gold-colored book from the back pocket of his jeans. The title — *The G.H.O.U.L. Guide* — was embossed on the spine, and from the front protruded the face of its author, Samuel Skipstone.

"Did you hear what happened, Mr. Skipstone?" Luke asked.

The face on the cover of the book opened its eyes. "Indeed I did," confirmed the author, "and I have to admit that I do not know why the doorway has remained open. But I think you are wise to maintain an air of caution."

Samuel Skipstone was one of Scream Street's founding fathers, and he had spent his life researching and cataloging the community and its residents. At the time of his death, he cast a spell to merge his spirit with the pages of his book, *Skipstone's Tales of Scream Street,* where he had resided until only yesterday, when he had moved into his new home, *The G.H.O.U.L. Guide.*

"You know, now that I think of it, there is a bit of a family resemblance!" Resus said, looking from Luke to the book and back again. Only the day before, Luke had been amazed to learn that Samuel Skipstone was actually his great-great-great-great-great-great-grandfather. The werewolf gene, although present in Skipstone, had remained dormant for several generations until Luke had started to transform.

"We don't know why the doorway is still working even though the relics have been separated," Cleo explained. "We split them up among ourselves as souvenirs."

"My guess is that it has to do with self-preservation," said the author. "The relics may have increased their magical potential since the doorway was formed."

Resus pulled the vampire's fang from his cloak and stared at it. "You mean these things are alive?"

"They are now each saturated with the combined power of Scream Street's founding fathers," explained Skipstone. "I would suggest that they have developed the ability to adapt to new challenges."

Luke breathed a sigh of relief. "So that means we don't have to keep the relics here to make sure the doorway stays open for my mom."

"Very true," responded Skipstone, "but it does raise another pressing question. . . . How will you close the doorway once your mother has returned?"

Luke paused, then looked to Resus and Cleo for an answer. They both shrugged.

"You mean there's a possibility that other people could come through the doorway and into Scream Street, just like Steven Black did?" asked the mummy.

"It is more of a likelihood than a possibility," replied the face on the book solemnly.

"That's not good," said Resus. "I don't like the idea of anyone from Luke's world being able to just wander in and out of Scream Street whenever they like."

"Then we'll have to find a way to deactivate the relics and close the doorway," said Cleo. "And soon!"

Resus sighed. "Just when I was looking forward to a bit of peace and quiet."

"Would there be anything in your research that could show us how to do that, Mr. Skipstone?" Luke asked. "How to switch off the power of the relics?"

"It is possible," said Skipstone. "Although, do not forget, my life's work turned to ash when

I left it to provide you with the final relic in your quest."

This was true. When the trio had reversed the author's spell and returned Samuel Skipstone's spirit to his rotting body, *Skipstone's Tales of Scream Street,* the book in which he had spent the previous two centuries, had disintegrated in front of their eyes.

"You must have made notes, though," said Cleo in a flash of inspiration. "Your old house is filled with stacks and stacks of paper and notebooks—maybe something there could help us!"

"The answer to our problem could possibly be found there," agreed Samuel Skipstone, "but I would be unable to undertake the task alone. Perhaps I could impose upon the three of you to assist me in my research."

"Will we get time off to run to Everwell's to buy snacks?" asked Resus.

Skipstone smiled. "I am sure that could be arranged."

"Then count me in!"

Luke glanced nervously at the shimmering doorway leading to his old street. "Are you sure we can leave this unguarded?" he asked.

"The sooner we find a way to close it, the less likely it is that normals will stumble upon it and find their way into Scream Street," Cleo pointed out.

"I suppose so," Luke agreed reluctantly. "Although I can't say I'm looking forward to sifting through all that paperwork!" He slipped *The G.H.O.U.L. Guide* back into his pocket and followed Resus and Cleo across the square toward Samuel Skipstone's old house.

Had they looked back, the trio would have noticed the glowing tip of a cigar in the shadows of a nearby yard. Someone had been listening.

Chapter Three

The Problem

Luke sat upright as the first rays of morning sunshine streamed through the windows of 1 Scream Street and woke him. He had been curled up on the floor among stacks of papers, and someone must have thrown an old blanket over him while he slept. As he pushed the blanket away, he was enveloped in a thick cloud of dust. He sneezed.

"Sorry," said Cleo, appearing beside him. "It was the only blanket I could find. Mr. Skipstone's bed was pretty filthy."

Resus was sitting at Samuel Skipstone's desk, his head resting on his arms, his eyes closed, and his cape wrapped around his shoulders. "At least he *got* a blanket," Resus grumbled.

"I thought you were still asleep," observed Cleo.

The young vampire sat up and rubbed his eyes. "I was until Luke started sneezing!" *The G.H.O.U.L. Guide* lay silently on the desk in front of him.

"Did we find out how to close the doorway?" asked Luke, climbing to his feet and beginning to sift through the notes on the desk.

"*We?*" snorted Resus with a laugh. "*We* didn't do anything. You crashed out before midnight, you lightweight!"

"Well, you were snoring away twenty minutes later," Cleo teased. She turned back to Luke and shook her head. "Nothing yet."

"So it can't be closed?" said Luke.

"There is *one* possible course of action . . ." began Samuel Skipstone, opening his eyes. "But I doubt you'll want to take it."

Luke picked up the golden book from the desk. "What do you mean?" he asked.

"The doorway was opened for one reason only," explained the author. "To allow you and your parents to pass through and return to your former lives. Once that has happened, it will cease to exist."

"But we're staying in Scream Street now," said Luke. "We don't *want* to go back to our old lives."

"Then we must discover a way to disable the magic in the relics and force the doorway closed," said Skipstone. "It will not be an easy task, however; if the relics can now be separated from one another and the doorway, their power must be increasing."

Luke slumped into a chair, raising another cloud of dust as he did so. He coughed. "The founding fathers must have planned for something like this, surely," he said.

"Unfortunately not," replied Skipstone. "We

believed the relics would be gathered, then their power activated. We did not consider the outcome of the magic remaining unused."

"What about transforming one of the relics into something else?" suggested Resus. "The doorway closed when Count Negatov's fang was accidentally changed into a pair of glasses, remember."

"Trapping us in Luke's world," added Cleo with a shudder.

"I suspect that the relics will have already evolved past the stage at which that would work," replied Skipstone. "Although at present it is the only option we have — and therefore worth a try."

"Right," said Luke, standing up again and grabbing *The G.H.O.U.L. Guide* from the desk. "We'll need Eefa to do that for us. Will Everwell's Emporium be open yet?"

Resus pulled his watch from his cloak and held it up to see. "Just about," he said. "And a good thing, too — I can feel a rat sausage sandwich coming on. Let's go!"

"Is there ever a time when you're not desperate to stuff your face with the remains of some

poor, defenseless animal?" demanded Cleo as she followed the boys out into the hallway.

"Poor, *delicious* animal," corrected Resus, opening the front door and stepping outside. "And it's all right for you: you keep your stomach in the fridge—"

"There's some of them!" shouted a voice. A series of bright white flashes forced Resus to shield his eyes. When he looked up again, he was amazed to find a dozen or more people crowded around the front gate, taking photographs.

"It's a vampire!" cried one.

"Show us your fangs!"

"Drink some blood!"

More flashes exploded around them.

"There's another one there, too—wrapped in bandages."

"It must be a mummy! Get a picture of it, Dave."

Cleo cowered as another flash almost blinded her.

Luke pushed his friends aside and stormed down the walkway toward the group. "What's going on?" he demanded. "Who are you people?"

A large, middle-aged man in a checked suit

turned a video camera on Luke. "Who are you supposed to be, then? The one the vampire bites?"

Luke pressed his hand up against the lens. "Get that thing out of my face!"

A surly woman who looked as though she might be the man's wife grabbed Luke's wrist and pulled it away. "Don't you touch that," she snarled. "We paid to get in, so we'll film what we like!"

Luke paled. *"Paid?"* he asked quietly. "But . . ."

Resus joined him, and there was another volley of flashes. "Come on," he said. "Let's get out of here."

"Are there more like you?" asked a skinny teenager.

"Where are they?"

"Have you got monsters here, too?"

Resus opened the gate and pushed Luke through the jostling crowd, clutching Cleo's hand and dragging her with him. As they headed for the central square, further comments rang in their ears:

"They weren't very good, were they?"

"I hope the rest of this place is better."

When the trio of friends reached the edge

of the square, they froze, hardly able to believe their eyes. It was packed with men, women, and children—noisy sightseeing families everywhere, taking photographs and shooting videos.

"They're . . . They're all *normals*!" Cleo gasped.

An angry shout echoed across the square as the door to 11 Scream Street crashed open. Twinkle the fairy, his potbelly bulging over the top of his frilly pink tutu, emerged, carrying a scrawny man under his thick, tattooed arm. "Get out of my house and stay out!" he shouted, tossing the man onto the lawn.

The man leaped to his feet and began rubbing the grass stains from his pants. "You can't stop me. I bought a season ticket!"

"Don't make me angry," growled the fairy. Then he stomped back into his house and slammed the door behind him.

A bat whipped over Cleo's head, screeching wildly. "Isn't that the bat from the emporium?" she asked.

The trio turned just in time to see Eefa Everwell push a handful of people out of her shop. "You are *not* allowed to touch anything in there!" she yelled, forcing the door closed against them.

Dr. Skully's skeletal dog, Scapula, appeared at Resus's feet, trembling and whining miserably. "Where's his tail?" asked the vampire.

"Those kids have got it!" exclaimed Cleo, spotting a group of giggling boys playing with a piece of bone. She marched over and snatched it from their hands. "I'll take that."

She turned to return the tail, and as she did so, one of the boys grabbed a hold of a loose bandage and pulled hard. "You look like you had an accident," he taunted.

Cleo stepped up to him. "It'll be *you* who has the accident if you don't knock it off," she growled.

Laughing, the boys ran away just as Doug lurched into view, pursued by a young man, shouting, "At least let me give you some money for a cup of coffee!"

"This is bad," said Resus as the chaos continued around them. "Very bad."

Suddenly they spotted a familiar face among the crowd. Scream Street's landlord, Sir Otto Sneer, was ushering people through the rainbow-colored doorway. At the head of the line was his nephew, Dixon, wearing a sandwich board that read: *Follow me to visit the greatest freak show on earth*.

"This way to the freaks!" Sir Otto bellowed as he collected payment from the new arrivals. "Ghosts and ghouls on every corner! Scares and screams guaranteed!"

"What's he talking about?" asked Cleo. "What's going on?"

Luke felt a knot tighten in his stomach. "We're being invaded!"

Chapter Four
The Confrontation

Luke pushed through the groups of tourists and strode toward the landlord, Resus and Cleo hot on his heels.

"Line up! Line up!" chanted Sir Otto as yet more visitors stepped through the shimmering archway. "Just thirty dollars each to visit the greatest freak show on earth!"

"You can't do this, Sneer," called Luke as he and his friends approached.

Sir Otto bit down on his cigar and grinned at them. "Oh, but I can," he crowed, beaming and stroking the white silk scarf around his neck. "These are *my* houses, and if I want to charge people to come and see them, that's what I'll do."

He paused to accept a bundle of bills from an eager family that had just appeared through the doorway, then stuffed the money into a leather bag hanging from his belt. "Welcome to Scream Street, where the entertainment never ends!" he announced.

Sir Otto's nephew slid out of his sandwich board and hopped excitedly from foot to foot. "Entertainment?" he exclaimed. "Will there be a show, Uncle Otto?"

"You idiot, Dixon," barked the landlord. "And it's *Sir* Otto."

"Sorry, *Sir* Uncle Otto," said Dixon. "But will it be a musical, or a play? I hope it's a play— I like to think of myself as the cultured type."

The landlord slapped his nephew across the back of the head. "And I like to think of you as the *injured* type!" he said with a smirk, turning

back to the line of visitors. "Thirty dollars each, folks," he called, accepting payment from yet another family and pushing it into his money bag. "The residents are in good form today. In fact, you could say they're *dying* to meet you!"

Luke fumed as this latest group set off to explore. "You won't get away with this!"

"Get away with what?" The landlord chortled. "It was *you* who opened the doorway, boy." He grinned widely and blew cigar smoke in Luke's face. "All I'm doing is capitalizing on *your* hard work!"

Unable to hold himself back, Luke lunged for Sir Otto, lashing out with his hand to knock the cigar from his mouth. Instead, his fingers caught the scarf around his neck and pulled it away, revealing scarred skin and ripped tissue underneath. This was the result of an attack on Sir Otto during his childhood, and, self-conscious of the wound, the landlord quickly pulled his jacket closed to conceal it. "You've just earned your family a spot on the guided tour," he growled.

Resus snatched the scarf from Luke and threw it back at the landlord. "Come on," he said to his friend. "Let's go."

"But I can't let him . . ." began Luke.

"Resus is right," said Cleo. "This isn't the time or the place."

"I'll surround you with paying customers night and day," Sir Otto threatened as the trio walked away. "If I can't rid this street of freaks, I'll put you to good use and earn a fortune from you."

"Well, *my* money won't be a part of it," declared a voice. "This place is boring—I demand a full refund!"

Luke, Resus, and Cleo turned to see the surly woman march up to Sir Otto as he hurriedly replaced the silk scarf around his neck.

"Madam," said the landlord, "perhaps you didn't read the fine print on the back of your ticket. Refunds cannot be given under any circumstances."

"I don't read anything I don't have to, finely printed or not!" snapped the woman. "You promised me a street full of freaks, and all I've seen so far are a few cheap costumes and some lame special effects."

People around them stopped what they were doing to listen to the woman's complaints as her voice rose above the general din.

41

"There are no costumes *here,* madam!" exclaimed Sir Otto. "I assure you that everything you see is the genuine article."

"Come off it," snarled the woman. "I've been to scarier tea parties!"

A man with a thin mustache joined the group slowly building up around Sir Otto. "That shopkeeper wouldn't let my family inside to buy souvenirs," he complained.

"The 'zombie' you sent me to look at was nothing more than a tramp," said another voice.

"I want my money back!"

"Me, too!"

The trio looked on as the normals continued to argue with Sir Otto.

"I thought we were going," said Cleo.

"What, and miss Sneer trying to squirm his way out of this?" Luke said.

Resus pulled a steaming paper bag from inside his cloak. "Popcorn, anyone?"

Sir Otto began to back away as the crowd closed in around him, all now demanding their money back. "B-but, this entire street is packed with weirdoes and oddities," he stammered.

The surly woman planted her hands on her hips. "Prove it," she said mockingly.

The landlord grabbed his nephew by the scruff of the neck and dragged him into the middle of the mob. "Show them what you can do," he commanded.

Luke's grin quickly faded. Dixon was a shape-shifter, with the ability to transform into any living creature he chose. Once he revealed his extraordinary power, the tourists would have no doubt about Sir Otto's claims that Scream Street was packed with abnormal residents.

"Come on, you moron," Sir Otto yelled. "Show them!"

A hush fell over the crowd as Dixon stepped forward. He cleared his throat, struck a theatrical pose, and proclaimed:

> "I put my goldfish on the floor,
> He isn't very fit.
> He only did ten sit-ups,
> Then lay still—that was it!"

Nobody spoke for a few moments. The angry tourists shuffled their feet, and Luke, Resus, and Cleo exchanged confused glances.

Dixon, taking the silence as a good sign, raised his face to the sun and continued:

> "I used my cat
> As a bike crash-hat

And tied him to my head.
The road had a lump,
I fell off with a bump,
And now my cat's a bit dead!"

Sir Otto, his face slowly turning purple, let out a low, gurgling scream. "What, in the name of all that's wicked, are you *doing*?" he shrieked.

Dixon swallowed hard but stood his ground. "You s-seem to think, dear uncle, that I cannot be cultured. Well, I have been perfecting my art alone in my room for the past few weeks, and now it is time to offer myself to the public." He paused dramatically. "I am a poet!"

"You're wasting our time," shouted the surly woman. "I want my money!"

Sir Otto looked as if he might explode. He grabbed Dixon by the ears and pulled his face up against his own, the burning tip of his cigar threatening to slide up his nephew's left nostril. "You are *not* a poet," he growled. "You are a shapeshifter. Now, do what I tell you and change into a banshee or a goblin and get these cretins off my back!"

"You'd better give us *cretins* a refund now,

before we take it from you by force!" yelled another angry voice as the crowd pushed forward once again.

"Dixon!" roared Sir Otto. "Do something!" His ginger-haired nephew took a deep breath and began another verse:

"I wandered lonely as a clown . . ."

As the irritated visitors continued to demand their money back, Sir Otto caught sight of Luke, Resus, and Cleo laughing hysterically.

"This is awesome," Cleo said, giggling.

"I demand more of Dixon's poetry!" declared Resus.

"It's not as easy to exploit us as you thought, is it?" Luke called out to the landlord.

"There!" shouted Sir Otto, pointing desperately at Resus. "There's a vampire right there."

The surly woman glanced over her shoulder at the trio. "Don't try that nonsense with me," she scowled. "Anyone can dress a kid up in a vampire cloak and stick a pair of plastic fangs in his mouth!"

Right on cue, Resus pulled out his fake fangs and held them up. "She's not wrong, Otto."

"The mummy, then," bellowed Sir Otto. "Look at the mummy!"

Cleo made a miserable face. "The nasty man said he'd punish me if I didn't let him wrap me up in bandages," she wailed.

"The boy!" Sir Otto roared finally. "That annoying, self-satisfied brat of a boy. He's a werewolf. If I'm lying, I'll give everyone *double* their money back!"

As one, the crowd turned to glare greedily in Luke's direction.

"The best thing is—you don't even have to wait for a full moon!" Sir Otto Sneer puffed on his cigar and gave a malevolent smile. "All you have to do is make him angry."

Chapter Five
The Plan

The crowd slowly advanced upon Luke.
"Make him angry enough, and he'll transform
into a werewolf," Sir Otto reminded them.

Luke began to back away. "What are you doing?" he exclaimed. "Two minutes ago, you were demanding a refund!"

"A refund he'll double once we prove you're not a werewolf," said the woman, pointing to Sir Otto.

"He's *not* a werewolf," insisted Resus, stepping forward. "Really, he isn't!"

"Why should we take *your* word for it?" asked a man near the front of the crowd. "You tried to fool us into thinking you were a real vampire!"

"Please stop," pleaded Cleo.

"Butt out, little girl!" warned the surly woman.

"I think we'd better get out of here," hissed Resus, catching Luke's and Cleo's eyes. Luke grabbed Cleo's hand, and, without a moment's hesitation, the trio turned and ran as fast as they could across the square.

"Forget double refunds," bellowed Sir Otto. "The reward for the first person to make that freak transform is a thousand bucks!" Without needing a second invitation, the crowd quickly gave chase.

"I'll make Sneer pay for this!" cried Luke, his feet pounding against the concrete.

"Try to stay calm," said Cleo. "He *wants* you to get angry, remember?"

"Yeah," agreed Resus. "Once those normals get a glimpse of your werewolf, they'll never go home!"

The trio had almost reached the other side of the square when a camera bag came flying through the air toward them. The strap caught around Luke's ankle, tripping him up and bringing him crashing to the ground. The crowd was upon him in seconds.

"Make him angry!" shouted the surly woman. "I want that reward!" She kicked Luke sharply in the leg. He yelled out in pain and clutched at his shin.

"Think calm thoughts," commanded Resus, pulling his friend to his feet as the normals jostled them around. "Don't let them get to you!"

But it was too late—Luke's anger was building, and the rage already flowed through his veins. He threw back his head and howled as werewolf fangs burst through his gums, pushing his own teeth to one side.

"He's changing!" hissed Cleo.

"We can't let them see him like this," said

Resus, and he swiftly unclipped his cloak and threw it over Luke's head just as the first few patches of brown fur began to appear.

"They're hiding him!" shouted a furious voice.

"Get that cape off!" roared another.

As the crowd tried to pull the cloak away, Luke's transformation continued in the shadows beneath it.

"What are we going to do?" wailed Cleo.

"Whatever it is, we'd better do it fast," replied Resus, trying to restrain the struggling figure. "He's in the mood to tear someone to pieces!"

"Hey!" hollered a gruff voice above them. "Up here!"

Cleo and Resus looked up, and to their amazement, they saw Twinkle hovering above the crowd, his tiny wings flapping to keep him aloft. The hefty fairy reached a plump arm down to them.

"Tie 'im up wiv summink," ordered Twinkle.

"Fairy 'nuff!" quipped Resus, grinning with relief.

Cleo quickly unwrapped a length of bandage from her leg, which Resus wound around Luke's writhing form. Then he tossed the other end

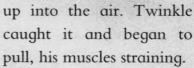

up into the air. Twinkle caught it and began to pull, his muscles straining.

Resus and Cleo in turn clung to Luke, and Twinkle lifted the three of them off the ground. The angry crowd stared up in astonishment.

"I warned you," grunted Twinkle as he carried Luke, Resus, and Cleo up into the air and away over the rooftops. "Never mess wiv an angry fairy!"

"They're still out there," Resus reported, leaving the window and slumping into one of the huge plush sofas in Mr. and Mrs. Crudley's fancy living room.

"They'll be looking for me so they can claim that reward," Luke said with

a sigh, resting his feet on the edge of the coffee table. "I doubt they'll go anywhere while there's still a grand up for grabs."

One of the pulsating bog monsters slithered over and knocked Luke's feet off the table. "Do you mind?" she gurgled. "It's bad enough that I've had to invite so many people into my home, without you giving me extra housework!" She wiped at an invisible shoeprint, slopping tendrils of slime from her own arm over the furniture as she did so. Luke obediently tucked his feet under the table.

"How are you doing?" Cleo asked him quietly.

"I don't know," admitted Luke. "I really thought I was starting to control my transformations — but this one was all wrong."

"How do you mean?"

"I don't usually transform fully unless I decide to," said Luke. "Recently I've been able to choose which part of my body changes. But this time I just lost it."

Cleo patted his arm comfortingly. "It was just the crowd," she assured him. "All the noise and the way they were pushing you around.

You've never had to deal with anything like that before."

Luke fell silent. Twinkle had taken him, Resus, and Cleo back to 13 Scream Street, where Luke's parents had helped to lock him in his bedroom until his transformation reversed. While the werewolf was out of harm's way, Resus and Cleo had spread the word about an urgent residents' meeting that night. The Crudleys' house had been chosen because it had the largest rooms.

"Well, I don't see why these children had to open that ridiculous doorway in the first place," spluttered Mr. Crudley, spraying goo all over a nearby tree nymph as he spoke.

Luke's mom stood to face him. "They did it for us," she retorted. "So Luke could take us back to our old lives."

"Then I suggest he does exactly that," said the bog monster. "Once you're through that doorway, it will close behind you and we'll all be left in peace!"

"We're not going anywhere," insisted Mr. Watson, jumping to his wife's defense. "Luke belongs in Scream Street just as much as you do."

Mr. Crudley's watery yellow eyes narrowed. "Maybe *he* belongs here," he gargled, "but you two don't. You're normals, just like those others out there."

"Now, you wait a minute—"

"Dudes!" yelled a voice as Doug lurched into the fray. "Let's keep things in the spirit of friendship here." He smiled to reveal a family of cockroaches scuttling around his teeth. "Share the love, man."

"Doug has a point," agreed Dr. Skully. "If we start fighting among ourselves, we're no better than the people outside that window."

"I found the bat from Everwell's cowering in my underwear drawer," said Diana Howl, Simon Howl's wife. "The poor thing was terrified!"

Dr. Skully sighed, and as he did so, the bones of his rib cage rose and fell. "And they dare to call *us* monsters . . ."

"I want to know why G.H.O.U.L. isn't helping us," said Eefa Everwell. "Why can't it get rid of the normals?"

Zeal Chillchase stepped suddenly out of the shadows. "So far, this situation has avoided the attention of G.H.O.U.L.," he said calmly.

 55

Resus shuddered and leaned in to Luke. "I wish he'd stop appearing like that!" he whispered.

"I can help only in an unofficial capacity," Chillchase continued. "If I were to ask it for help, G.H.O.U.L. would almost certainly banish the children to the Underlands for using the relics to open the doorway, thus breaching the rules of Scream Street."

"Good riddanssse to them, I sssay," hissed a snakelike creature from the back of the room. "The wolf-boy can take hisss normal parentsss with him, too!"

"The Watsons are staying right here," announced Bella Negative. "They're our neighbors, and our friends. Besides, we can't close the doorway with so many normals still in Scream Street. They'd be trapped here."

"It would serve them right for the way they've behaved," declared Simon Howl. A handful of other residents applauded his comment.

"But we don't *want* the normals here!" rumbled Mr. Crudley, spitting slime down the front of his vest. "They're vile, disgusting creatures!"

"So we need to find a way to get rid of them before we close the doorway," said Resus's mom.

"And I think Luke should be the one to decide what we do next."

Luke looked surprised. "Why me?" he asked.

"Because you had the strength and the courage to help your parents in the first place," said Bella kindly. "We should be able to trust you to help the rest of us."

"I don't see what I can do," admitted Luke. "The minute I step outside, they'll attack me again! I just wish things would go back to normal."

"That's it!" exclaimed Resus.

"It is?" asked Luke.

"You saw how they reacted when they thought Sir Otto was running some sort of scam," replied Resus excitedly. "They couldn't wait to get their money back and leave. So we just have to convince them that we're *all* normals! That way, they'll think visiting Scream Street just isn't worth the money."

"How can we do that?" asked Cleo. "They saw Twinkle fly!"

"We could make them think he was attached to wires," suggested Alston.

"Brilliant!" said Resus.

"What about the houses?" asked Simon Howl. "Everything around here is twisted and terrifying to them—we can't disguise all that."

"If anyone asks, we can say we're waiting for a government grant to fix the place up," said Luke. "The normals will just be too pleased they don't live anywhere as run-down as this to question it further."

"But what about the rest of us?" asked Dr. Skully. "Some of us don't exactly look or act like normals."

Mr. Watson stood up, his eyes twinkling. "Just leave that to me."

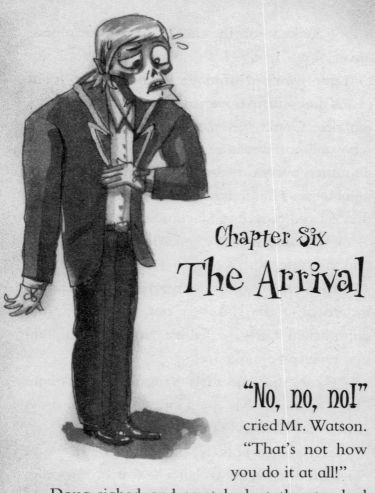

Chapter Six
The Arrival

"No, no, no!"
cried Mr. Watson.
"That's not how
you do it at all!"
Doug sighed and scratched at the starched
collar buttoned around his neck. He was dressed
in one of Mr. Watson's old work suits and had
even allowed Tibia Skully to wash the dried
blood, dirt, and dead insects out of his hair. With

a little makeup on his cheeks, he looked almost alive.

Luke watched from the corner of the room as his dad scurried over to give Doug some acting tips. Could this really be the same person who only a few weeks ago had almost lost consciousness every time he saw one of their unusual neighbors? Things had certainly changed since they'd been moved to Scream Street.

"OK," said Mr. Watson, "let's try it again—and this time, with feeling!"

Frowning in concentration, Doug crossed the room, trying his best not to stagger, and approached Berry, a female zombie, who had also received a makeover.

"Dude," he began. Mr. Watson gave a cough. "Er, I mean . . . My good lady, would you be so kind as to tell me the time?"

Berry smiled politely, pulled up the sleeve of her blouse to reveal a delicate watch, and said, "Brains!"

"Stop, stop!" ordered Mr. Watson. "I have not spent six years as the lead in my local amateur dramatic company for nothing! I want you both to go and work on your characters." As the

zombies lurched away, shamefaced, he called, "Next!"

Mr. Crudley slithered into view, a trail of brown gloop staining the carpet behind him. A small bowler hat was perched on his massive, blubbery head.

"And what are you supposed to be?" Mr. Watson asked.

"I'm the man about town," replied the bog monster. "Your average, everyday man on the street."

"You don't think you look more like an average, everyday compost heap?"

"How dare you?" demanded Mr. Crudley. "Some of my best friends are compost heaps — but *they* don't carry umbrellas."

"Er, you're not carrying an umbrella. . . ."

"Yes, I am!" spluttered the mound of mud and goo. "It's right . . . Ah, now, where is it?" He plunged his fist into his slimy side and eventually pulled out a broken umbrella.

"I think you and your wife had better remain indoors until all this is over," Mr. Watson suggested tactfully. Mr. Crudley sludged away, muttering.

"Are you ready for us now, Dad?" called Luke from his spot in the corner.

"OK," said Mr. Watson. "Although I'm not holding out much hope."

Luke indicated for Resus to bring his parents into the room, and Mr. Watson gasped. The difference was astonishing. All three vampires had exchanged capes for jeans and sweaters, and Resus had washed off his pale makeup and even spiked his hair with gel.

"You look amazing!" cried Luke's dad. "Do you think you'll be able to keep up the pretense that you're normals?"

Neither Alston nor Bella Negative replied; they simply smiled sweetly, their mouths firmly closed.

"I said, do you think you'll be able to convince the normals that you're just like them?" asked Mr. Watson.

Silence.

"Mom and Dad can't speak, or they'll show their fangs," explained Resus. "Unlike me, they can't just take them out for a while!"

"And we were able to mix sunblock into their makeup," added Luke. "That way, they can go outside in daylight for long periods of time, just like everyone else."

"Good thinking," said his dad approvingly. "And now it's time to put everyone to the test."

The next morning, Luke headed out into Scream Street, quickly pulling up the hood of his sweat-shirt. He didn't want any normals recognizing him and trying to make him transform again.

Resus bounced along beside him in Luke's spare sneakers. "How can you walk in these things?" he hissed. "It's like being on springs!"

"It's only for a little while, just until we get the normals out of here," Luke assured him. "Then you can go back to dressing like a ball-room dancer!"

"We still have to work out how to close the doorway," Resus reminded him, ignoring the jibe. "Let's deal with one problem at a time, shall we?"

As the boys entered the square, they surveyed the scene before them. The residents of Scream Street were mingling with the normal tourists, each trying to remain inconspicuous. Sir Otto, standing at the shimmering doorway, scowled whenever one of them passed him.

Dr. Skully, his frame covered by a long rain-coat and his skull hidden by an oversize hat, was out walking Scapula, who was wrapped in lengths of fake fur cut from one of Mrs. Crudley's coats. The bog monster had had to be physically held back as Cleo snipped out the shapes, but it was worth it.

Doug, Turf, and Berry were merrily digging up the flower beds in a nearby garden. They had wanted to continue with their scene where they asked passersby for the time, but Luke had told them that he'd buried a nice, juicy liver, and now there was no holding them back.

"You don't think Twinkle's being a bit obvious, do you?" asked Resus, watching the crowd gathered outside 11 Scream Street. The fairy had set up a homemade trapeze and, dressed in the leotard of a circus high-wire performer, was busy giving out handwritten leaflets that read:

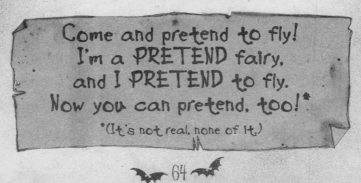

Come and pretend to fly!
I'm a PRETEND fairy,
and I PRETEND to fly.
Now you can pretend, too!*
*(It's not real, none of it.)

Luke grinned and turned his attention to Everwell's Emporium. "Let's go and see how Cleo's doing."

The boys pushed open the silver doors to Scream Street's general store and found the place packed with tourists. Instead of purchasing crystal balls and spell books, however, the normals were browsing shelves filled with as many boring, everyday items as the residents had been able to find. Everwell's Emporium had been transformed into a junk shop. Tarnished silverware sat beside well-thumbed books, and a pair of teenagers were busy rifling through a box of Luke's old computer games.

"You might not get some of those back, you know," said Resus.

Luke nodded grimly. "But it'll be worth it."

Eefa was behind the counter, her enchantment charm removed for the occasion. She was dressed in drab overalls, and her usually silky hair was knotted and greasy.

The bat that always sat above the shop door and screeched to announce the arrival of new customers was locked in a cage, bright feathers tied to its wings and a cardboard beak strapped

in place to make it look like a parrot.

"There's Cleo," whispered Luke, pointing towards the storeroom at the back of the shop. The boys headed over and found their friend unpacking boxes of even more dull things to sell. Cleo was dressed in a huge teddy-bear costume, complete with a giant, furry head.

"Any chance of a cuddle?" Resus grinned.

The teddy bear glared in his direction. "I'll drop-kick you in a minute!" it snapped in a muffled voice.

Resus pretended to be scared, but Cleo ignored him and sat down heavily on one of the boxes. "I'm sweating like crazy in here," she groaned. "My bandages are soaked!"

"Well, it was either wear that or stay hidden indoors," said Luke. "There's no other way to hide your face."

"Where did you get this thing, anyway?" demanded the mummy.

"We did *Goldilocks and the Three Bears* as our school play when I was younger," explained Luke. "That's the baby-bear costume my mom made for me."

"Good thing, too," said Resus, smirking. "I

couldn't *bear* it if Cleo missed out on all this excitement!"

The giant teddy waddled across the storeroom as fast as it could and grabbed Resus by the scruff of his brightly colored sweater. "I've been up all night with Eefa, restocking these shelves with junk so we could open again this morning," Cleo growled. "I'm too tired for your stupid jokes."

"Well, if you're tired," said Luke, "why don't you *paws* for breath?"

Resus collapsed in a fit of giggles, tears running down his cheeks as he gave Luke a high-five. Cleo shook her giant bear head in exasperation and shot the boys a glare that was wasted on them.

A little girl passing the door to the storeroom tugged at her mom's sleeve. "I'm bored," she wailed. "Can we go home now?"

Her mother dropped the half-used tube of toothpaste back onto the shelf. "We might as well," she agreed. "There's nothing but junk here."

Luke leaned in to whisper through one of the bear's ears, "Looks like you might be out of there soon!" And, taking a fluffy paw each, he and Resus led Cleo through the shop and out into the

square. A stream of normals was heading deject-
edly toward the rainbow-colored doorway.

"It's working," said Resus as Sir Otto tried
desperately to convince the crowds not to leave.
"Scream Street is almost ours again!"

He had barely finished speaking when an
excited yell rang out and a young vampire, age
around six or seven, skipped into the square, his
black cape flapping out behind him.

"Hello," he called, his tiny fangs glinting in
the sunshine. "I'm a vampire!"

"No, you're not," retorted one of the tourists
already trudging for the exit. "You're just a kid in
a costume."

"Oh, yeah?" said the young vampire. "Then
how come I can do *this*?" And, leaping into the
air, he whipped his cape around his face with a
flourish. There was a puff of black smoke, then,
in full view of everyone, he turned into a bat.

Chapter Seven
The Transformation

Luke stared at the tiny black bat flapping around in the middle of the square. "How did he *do* that?"

"We can all do that," said Resus. "Well, *I* can't, obviously, but all *real* vampires can change into bats whenever they want."

Luke was stunned. "I've never seen your mom or dad in bat form before."

"There's no real reason for them to change," explained Resus. "Vampires developed it originally as a way to escape from men with big wooden stakes — and that's not really an issue here. Plus, bats are blind, and the older you get, the longer it takes for your eyesight to return."

Cleo pulled off the teddy-bear head and gulped down deep breaths of fresh air. "I haven't seen that kid around before."

Resus quickly grabbed the head and tried to jam it back on. "Don't take it off," he exclaimed. "You'll give the game away!"

"I think it might be a bit late for that," said Luke.

The crowds who had been about to go through the doorway were now dashing back into the square, their eyes on the newly transformed bat and their cameras back in their hands.

In a second puff of smoke, the bat transformed back into the child vampire. "*Told* you I was real," he announced.

"That must mean they're all real!" cried a voice.

The surly woman, back for a second visit, pushed her way to the front of the newly gathered

crowd. "Then I'm going to find that werewolf and get my reward."

"A reward!" exclaimed the crowd.

"He must be in disguise somewhere," called one person.

"Let's find him!" bellowed another.

The young vampire was soon lost in the stampede.

"He'll be crushed!" squealed Cleo.

"Not if I've got anything to do with it," said Resus, before remembering that he'd left his cape at home. "Looks like we're doing this the hard way," he sighed, and he and Luke began to push through the dozens of people around the small vampire. Meanwhile, Cleo was struggling to free herself from the teddy-bear costume.

All over the square, residents were running for cover. As Dr. Skully threw down Scapula's leash and raced for home, one of the normals saw him and gave chase. "That could be him—there, in the coat!" cried the man.

He lunged forward and grabbed Dr. Skully's raincoat, pulling it off to reveal the skeleton underneath—and dislodging one of the teacher's ribs in the process. The man stopped running

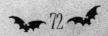

and scooped up the bone. "It might not be the werewolf," he said to himself, examining it, "but I bet I could get something for this on the Internet!"

Dr. Skully slowed to a halt when he realized that the man had given up the chase, only to find his way barred by a party of women.

"That's not the werewolf," declared one.

"I bet he can tell us where he is, though," answered a second.

One of them grabbed the skeleton and lifted him into the air. "Please, let me down," begged the teacher.

"Only when you tell us where to find the werewolf!"

Twinkle, giving up all pretense of being a circus performer, tore off his leotard to free his wings, rose into the air, and followed the sound of Dr. Skully's cries. He reached down into the throng with his massive fists, grabbed the teacher's skull, and pulled hard, his wings flapping furiously to keep him airborne. There was a *crack!* as the skull detached from the spine, sending the women sprawling.

"Let's go!" bellowed Twinkle.

What remained of Dr. Skully twisted around in the fairy's hands to look wistfully back toward the group. "My body!" he wailed.

Meanwhile, down in their yard, Doug, Turf, and Berry had abandoned their search for the liver and were instead scrabbling at the dirt in a bid to tunnel their way to safety.

A woman in high heels leaped over the hedge and caught hold of Doug's ankle just as he disappeared into the soil. "Oh, no, you don't!" she screeched. "Not until you tell me where the werewolf is."

Others joined her as she tried to drag the zombie back above ground. There was a sickening squelch as both of Doug's legs ripped free from his body, causing his pursuers to collapse backwards in a heap.

In the middle of the square, Resus dropped to his hands and knees in an attempt to reach the young vampire at the center of the crowd.

"Help me!" cried the small boy. "Help! Leave me alo—"

Then he suddenly fell quiet.

Luke, just a few feet away, was getting kicked and stepped on as he fought his own way through. "This is hopeless," he cried. He turned toward Resus. "Make sure you get him!" he yelled.

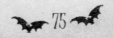

"Why?" Resus hollered back. "What are you going to do?"

"This!" declared Luke, forcing himself to his feet. He pulled back his hood. "WHY CAN'T YOU PICK ON A FREAK YOUR OWN SIZE?" he roared. Everyone stopped what they were doing. "I'm the one you *really* want!"

"It's the werewolf!" exclaimed a woman.

"He's mine!"

The crowd surged toward Luke, who battled his way free and raced off across the square, head down.

Up ahead, Dixon stood on a small box, reciting his poetry to anyone who would listen:

"I wish I was a coconut,
        Hanging on a palm.
Then I could drop on top of you
    And do your head some harm."

Luke charged past without so much as a backward glance.

Back in the middle of the square, Resus finally reached the small vampire, who was lying on the ground. Cleo skidded to a halt beside them.

"Is he OK?" she asked.

"A bit dazed, I think," replied Resus, helping the boy up. "Let's get him indoors." As they started toward the emporium, they could see more normals joining in the pursuit of Luke. Cleo gave a sharp intake of breath.

"We have to trust that he knows what he's doing," said Resus, struggling to run under the weight of the boy. "He probably just saved this kid's life."

Luke felt a stitch in his side as he continued to dodge his pursuers. He tried to stay calm; he had to keep his mind clear. This time, he wouldn't allow himself to be beaten.

He looked up: the tourists were beginning to close in from both sides. There was nothing to do but keep going straight ahead — toward the shimmering doorway of light.

That was it! If he could only get through the doorway and back into his own world, the normals would follow and leave Scream Street alone. He'd still have to lose the crowd on the other side, of course, but if he could find somewhere to hide, he could sneak back through when everything had calmed down.

Despite the pain in his side, Luke bent his head and sprinted for the rainbow-colored light. He could just about see his old street on the other side, the glistening barrier between the two worlds rippling like a wall of water. He was almost there. . . .

As he was about to step through the doorway, a large hand clamped around his throat and dragged him back into Scream Street, lifting him clear off the ground.

The face of Sir Otto Sneer appeared in his line of vision. "Nice try," it growled. Tossing Luke to the ground, the landlord yelled at the advancing crowd: "He's all yours!"

From the doorway of Everwell's Emporium, Resus and Cleo looked on as the normals surrounded Luke, pointing and poking at him as though he were some kind of laboratory specimen. Before they could do anything, they became aware of a figure dashing into the crowd. It was Luke's mom.

"LEAVE HIM ALONE!" screamed Mrs. Watson, trying to move the normals out of the way. "That's my son!" She dragged a teenager out by the hair and half pushed, half threw her to one side. Then, lashing out at a man in a baseball jacket, she managed to battle her way toward the center of the throng. "Luke!" she cried.

Finally she spotted him, crouching on the ground, his hands covering his face, and his legs kicking out against his attackers. She gave a final push forward, only to be grabbed by the hair and pulled backward.

"Stay back," snarled the surly woman, knocking Mrs. Watson off her feet. "That reward money is *mine*!"

Cleo and Resus dashed over to help, but they were stopped dead in their tracks. Mrs. Watson's nose was beginning to stretch and change shape, and long, sharp fangs were bursting through her gums.

Luke's mom was transforming into a were-wolf.

Chapter Eight
The Cage

Resus and Cleo watched the transformation, horrified. Mrs. Watson writhed on the ground as her spine twisted and her limbs began to lengthen. The snout was now completely stretched out, patches of dark-blond fur burst through her clothes, and a meaty tongue lolled between her jaws.

"What's going on?" cried Cleo.

Resus looked from the mummy to Luke's mom and back. "I would have thought that was perfectly obvious."

"No, I mean . . . I thought Luke was the only one in his family who could transform," said Cleo, unable to tear her eyes away.

"Maybe his mom had the werewolf gene in her all this time."

A long, furry tail ripped through the back of Mrs. Watson's pants.

"Maybe?" exclaimed Cleo.

"OK, then," said Resus, "she obviously *has* got it! But this must be the first time it's kicked in. It looks like it's going to be a full transformation, too."

"What should we do?" asked Cleo in a panic.

"We'll have to get *them* out of here," said Resus, glancing at the normals still crowded around Luke. "And quickly!"

"How?"

Finally, long talons sliced through Mrs. Watson's fingertips, and she raised her snout to the sky and howled.

The world seemed to pause for a few moments,

then chaos erupted. The tourists screamed as they ran, as one, from the werewolf.

"Well," said Resus, "that seems to have done the trick!"

Cleo rushed over to Luke and helped him to his feet. "We have to get out of here," she urged.

"Why?" he asked, lowering his hands from his face. "The normals have all—"

He stopped, the words stuck in his throat, as his mother's werewolf clambered to all fours and turned to face him, its eyes burning yellow. It growled.

"Oh, no," Luke whispered. He turned to Resus and Cleo, his eyes pleading. "Tell me that's not . . . ?"

"I'm afraid it is," said Cleo gently. "We have to go."

"I—I can't leave her," said Luke, backing away involuntarily as the werewolf came toward him. "That's my mom!"

"Not at the moment, it's not," said Resus as kindly as he could. "She could attack you."

"But . . ."

"I doubt you'll be able to reason with her when she's like this, Luke," said Cleo. "We used

 82

to try when you transformed, but it's not always possible."

"All you can do is wait for her to change back," added Resus.

Luke stared into what were no longer his mom's eyes. He couldn't bear to think about how scared she must be. He remembered the terror that had filled him when he had first transformed. He'd known something was happening, but—

Suddenly, without any warning, the werewolf sprang forward, teeth gnashing, toward Luke.

"Mom!" he cried, holding his hands up in front of him as though they could somehow protect him against the claws and fangs of this vicious beast. The wolf leaped . . . and sailed right over Luke, landing behind him with a snarl. It had another victim in mind.

The surly woman who had kick-started the riot stood trembling behind a hedge. Some of the tourists had made straight for the doorway, but most had found a hiding spot, torn between fear of the wolf and curiosity to see it in action.

"No!" screamed the woman, skidding on the grass as she tried to escape. She could hear the

werewolf's throaty growl and feel its hot breath on the back of her neck.

But before the creature could pounce, an object came sailing through the air and caught it on the side of the head. It was a leather money bag filled to the brim with coins. The werewolf fell, stunned by the blow.

"Run, while you still can!" Sir Otto ordered the woman, running over to collect his money bag.

"You hit my mom!" shouted Luke.

The landlord snarled. "She had to be stopped." He glanced up and caught sight of Cleo. "You — go and tell the Movers to bring my cage from Sneer Hall," he ordered.

"I'm not your messenger," retorted Cleo.

A deep growl built at the back of the wolf's throat as it began to come to.

"Do it!" shouted Sneer.

Luke stared deep into the wolf's eyes, hoping to find a glimmer of his mom in there. Nothing. "He's right, Cleo. We've got no choice," he said.

The mummy muttered something but nonetheless ran off in the direction of number 5 to seek the help of G.H.O.U.L.'s faceless assistants.

"Vampire," Sir Otto grunted at Resus, his

 84

eyes never leaving the werewolf, "in the shed on the grounds of Sneer Hall, there's a pole that I use to control my hellhounds. Dixon will show you where it is."

"Then why can't Dixon go and get it himself?" demanded Resus.

"Because I want someone to bring it here, not write a sonnet about it!"

Grumbling, Resus dashed off toward Sir Otto's mansion, pausing only to grab Dixon by the shirt and drag him along with him.

Sir Otto and Luke were left to face the wolf. Cowering normals watched on from various hiding places around the square, fascinated.

"Why are you doing this?" asked Luke. "Why are you saving people?"

"Call it financial sense," the landlord replied. "You can't pay if you're dead."

Luke gave a grim laugh. "I might have known it would be all about you!"

"You're in this, too," said Sir Otto. "You'll have to keep your mother occupied until the others get back."

"You want me to distract a werewolf?" asked Luke incredulously. "How?"

Sir Otto bit down hard on his cigar. "By doing what it is you freaks do best," he growled. "Be your freakish self."

Luke paled. "I—I can't change into a wolf to fight my own mom," he protested.

"Your choice," said Sneer flatly. The were-wolf raised its snout to the sky and gave a howl. "But if I were you, I wouldn't take too long to decide." With that, he kicked open the door to the house. Once inside, he slammed it closed, leaving Luke alone with the werewolf.

Saliva dripped from the creature's jaws as it turned to glare at Luke. He backed out of the garden and into the square, the wolf stalking his every move. If it attacked, there would be no way he could defend himself. His only chance in a fight would be if he transformed— but he couldn't bear the thought of hurting his mom.

"M-Mom," he stammered. "It's me—Luke!"

His words seemed to have no effect, and the wolf continued to advance.

Behind Luke, the first Movers arrived and began to assemble Sir Otto's cage. Cleo watched anxiously from the far side of the square.

Suddenly, the creature leaped. Before Luke could react, a metal loop was slipped over the blond werewolf's head, then tightened around its throat and jerked it backward. As the werewolf howled in anger and thrashed wildly, Resus and Dixon struggled to keep hold of the long metal pole to which the loop was attached.

"Get that cage ready!" bellowed Resus as Luke dashed over to help with the pole. The wolf howled in fury.

Finally, the Movers slotted the last remaining section into place: a heavy barred door. Resus and Dixon began to push Mrs. Watson's wolf toward the enclosure.

"Three, two, one . . . now!" shouted Resus.

Dixon released the catch to loosen the loop, then they slid the noose off the blond wolf's head and gave it a final shove before the Movers slammed the cage door shut with a *clang!* Sir Otto Sneer reappeared from his hiding place, ran over to the cage, and locked it with a small silver key, which he then slipped into the pocket of his jacket.

Luke and Resus sank to the ground, exhausted. Cleo scurried over and knelt beside them. "Are you OK?" she asked.

"I'm fine," said Luke, catching his breath.

"You did the right thing," said Resus. "At least your mom will be safe now until she changes back."

Mrs. Watson's werewolf hurled itself angrily at the bars of the cage again and again, but it held secure.

Sir Otto watched the werewolf for a moment, smiling to himself. Then he turned to the now

almost deserted square and bellowed, "Ladies and gentlemen!"

"What's he doing?" asked Luke as he and Resus climbed to their feet. All around them, normals were slowly beginning to emerge from their hiding places.

"You have all seen just how dangerous life on Scream Street can be," called the landlord. "Therefore, if you wish to stay, the price is now a mere two hundred dollars per person!"

Chapter Nine
The Boy

Excited normals crowded around Sir Otto, clamoring to be the first to give him fistfuls of cash.

"What are they *doing*?" demanded Cleo. "Can't they see how dangerous this place is for them? Why are they paying to stay?"

"That's exactly *why* they're paying to stay," said Resus sadly. "Some people will do anything for a thrill."

Luke watched as each of the tourists paid the additional fee to Sir Otto, then hurried over to the cage to take photographs of his mom's werewolf. At every pop of a flashbulb, the wolf howled in terror and threw itself against the bars of its cell.

Luke ran over to Sir Otto. "This is low, even for you."

The landlord grinned as he stuffed another handful of bills into his money bag. "I'm glad I haven't disappointed you. Now, shove off!"

"Not without the key to the cage," said Luke, holding out his hand.

Sir Otto roared with laughter. "And why would I give you that?"

"So I can let my mom out as soon as she changes back."

The werewolf growled as more and more normals crowded around its cage. "I can't see that happening any time soon," Sir Otto said.

Luke glared at him. "If you don't——"

Resus grabbed his friend by the arm and dragged him away. "Leave it," he said.

 91

Luke fought to free himself. "But I've got to help my mom!"

"We *will* help her," the vampire assured him. "We just have to wait for the right moment."

A family of normals were now daring each other to stand close enough to the cage to be able to get video footage of themselves alongside the snarling wolf.

"Couldn't you pick the lock with your nails?" Luke asked Resus in desperation.

"Then what?" demanded the vampire. "Open the door and let her eat me while you figure out where you're going to take her?"

"But I can't just leave her there. She's my mom!"

"You have to," said Cleo. "It's safer for everyone this way—including her."

"Luke!" cried a voice. Mr. Watson was hurrying across the square toward the trio. "I wondered where you were! I've been at Mr. and Mrs. Crudley's, trying to stop them from leaving the house—but I heard a commotion. Are you OK?"

Luke forced a thin smile. "I'm fine, Dad."

His dad looked relieved. "I can't find your mom anywhere, either. Have you seen her?"

Cleo and Resus exchanged glances. "Actually, she's —"

"She's with Dr. Skully," Luke interrupted quickly. "One of the normals recognized him and he lost a few bones. Mom's helping him to find them."

Mr. Watson surveyed the crowd in the square. "I figured something must have gone wrong," he said. "Still, it was worth a try." He gestured toward the werewolf, snapping at anyone who came within a few feet of its cage. "What's going on there?"

"Sneer got Dixon to shape-shift into a wolf," Luke lied. "They're using it as a trick to attract more visitors."

"Nasty man," muttered his dad. "OK, I'd better get back to babysitting the Crudleys. They'll be plucked apart and used as mud packs if they wander outside and this group spots them!" He began to make his way back toward the bog monsters' home. "If you see your mom, tell her I was looking for her."

"I will," Luke called after him.

"Why didn't you tell him?" asked Resus once Mr. Watson was out of earshot. "Why didn't you tell your dad what really happened to your mom?"

"He had a hard enough time coming to terms with *me* being a werewolf," said Luke quietly. "Seeing my mom that way would send him right over the edge."

"He's bound to find out sooner or later," said Cleo, "now that she's started transforming."

Luke shook his head. "Once she transforms back, it won't happen again."

"You don't know that," Resus pointed out.

"It *won't* happen again!" said Luke angrily. "Even if I have to stay with her twenty-four hours a day to stop her from getting angry."

"That's ridi—"

"We'll help you," Cleo said quickly, giving Resus a warning look. "We'll help to keep your mom calm so it doesn't happen again."

Luke stared unhappily at the werewolf, still pacing around its cage. "Thank you."

Suddenly, the surly woman appeared, her clothes ripped and covered in dirt, her face as white as a sheet. Twigs and leaves stuck out from her hair. "Y-You're the werewolf," she stammered as she caught sight of Luke.

"I'm *one* of them," he replied sourly.

"M–My reward . . . ?"

"Your reward is that you're still alive," snarled Cleo. "Unless you want him to transform as well?"

"Grrr!" growled Resus under his breath.

A low moan escaped from the woman's lips, and her skin seemed to grow even paler. She ran shakily for the doorway out of Scream Street.

Even Luke couldn't resist laughing. "I wouldn't like to have *her* nightmares tonight," he said.

Cleo gazed around her at the crowds still filling the square. "And to think, all this was started by a little boy!"

"I'd forgotten all about him," admitted Luke.

"I hadn't," said Resus. "I'd like to know what he's doing here. Let's go and find him."

The trio set off toward the emporium. As they approached, Eefa appeared in the shop doorway. "I was just about to come looking for you three," she smiled. "Your little friend is feeling better."

"Thank goodness," said Cleo. "Is he up to talking yet?"

Eefa rolled her eyes. "You could say that."

"I'm a vampire!" the boy declared.

Since Resus had left him, the boy had been skipping around Everwell's Emporium, telling Eefa about his family's history.

"Yes, we *know* you're a vampire," said Resus through gritted teeth. "You've told us at least a dozen times — and it's still not impressing me. I'm a vampire, too."

The boy looked at Resus in his jeans and sweater. "You don't *look* like a vampire," he said.

"It's my afternoon off."

"What's your name?" asked Cleo.

"Kian," replied the boy. "Kian the vampire!"

"Nice to meet you, Kian," said Cleo. "I'm Cleo, and this is—"

"What's wrong with him?" asked Kian, pointing to Luke, who was staring silently out of the window across the square. "He looks sad."

"He *is* sad," said Cleo. "Some people were mean to his mom."

"Why?"

Cleo took a deep breath. "Because she's a werewolf, and they haven't seen one of those before," she explained.

"And they still wouldn't have if you hadn't performed your little bat trick in front of them," grumbled Resus under his breath.

"Wow! His mom's a werewolf?" exclaimed Kian, wide eyed in astonishment. "I'm a vampire."

"If you tell us one more time . . ."

"Some men took *my* mom away," said Kian matter-of-factly. Resus stopped in his tracks. "They came and dragged her from our house."

Luke turned from the window. "When was this?"

"A few days ago," said Kian. "I don't know how long ago exactly, because I hid in the cellar until they stopped looking for me as well."

Cleo looked surprised. "Why were they looking for you?" she asked.

Kian shrugged. "They had fiery torches and sharp pieces of wood, so I don't think they wanted to be friends," he said.

"What happened next?" asked Resus in a friendlier tone.

"Then some different men came to the house," replied the small vampire. "They didn't say anything, but they looked much nicer."

"They're called Movers," explained Luke. "They came for me, too."

"I asked them if they knew where my mom was, but they couldn't hear me," said Kian. "They brought me here to a new house."

"You're here alone?" exclaimed Cleo.

"Oh, no." Kian smiled. "My grandpa already lives on Scream Street. I've come to stay with him—look!" He proudly showed them a purple wristband with the number 31 printed on it.

Luke rubbed his own wrist, where, waking

for the first time in his new home all those weeks ago, he too had found a purple band.

"There's another vampire on Scream Street?" asked Resus. "I didn't know that. What does your grandpa look like?"

"I don't know," said Kian. "I've never met him before, and I couldn't find him anywhere in the house when I woke up. He's a vampire."

"So, there'll just be you and him?" asked Luke.

"And my mom," Kian replied. "She'll come and live with us when she finds our new house— won't she?"

Cleo put her arm around the small vampire. "I'm sure she will," she said gently.

Resus reached out and took the boy's hand. "Until that happens, you come to me for anything you need," he said. "I live at number fourteen. My name's Resus Negative."

"That's my name, too!" Kian exclaimed.

"I don't think . . ." began Resus.

"It is! My name is Kian Negative—and I'm a vampire!"

Chapter Ten
The Lie

"He's definitely a Negative," agreed
Alston, lowering the vampire child's hand as he
lay asleep on the couch. "He has all the right
lines on his palm." Resus's dad, like the rest of his
family, had discarded his costume and returned to
wearing his cape.

Luke, Resus, and Cleo had brought Kian back to Resus's house to meet his parents, where, after an hour of constant chatter, the boy had eventually fallen sound asleep.

"Then how come we've never heard of him?" asked Resus. "If his grandpa's been living in Scream Street all this time, we'd know about it, wouldn't we?"

"Maybe he's not the socializing type," suggested Alston. "If he's elderly, he might prefer to stay indoors and keep to himself."

"Even if that's the case," said Resus, "I thought we were the only living descendents of Count Negatov."

"Count Negatov is the one we found in the sewers, isn't he?" asked Cleo. She recalled the moment when she, Luke, and Resus had pulled a fang from the mouth of an apparently dead vampire, only to discover that the founding father was still very much alive.

"Yep," said Resus. "But I don't know how Kian is connected to him."

"Perhaps I may be of assistance here," offered a muffled voice. Luke pulled *The G.H.O.U.L. Guide* from his pocket and propped it up on

a chair. Samuel Skipstone smiled out from its cover.

"Count Negatov had two sons," explained the author. "However, one left the family home at a young age and never returned. This was before the count helped to found Scream Street, of course."

"His son never joined him here?" said Alston. "Why not?"

"A feud over the inheritance of the family castle, I believe," replied Skipstone. "But that is all Count Negatov would ever tell me. I presume that this child and his grandfather are descended from the missing son."

"Which means that the grandfather has been living here under our very noses," added Alston.

Resus sat back in his chair. "So I guess that makes Kian a sort of cousin of mine," he said.

"A distant cousin," said Skipstone, "but a relative all the same. He and his mother appear to have settled in another part of the world, and had they not been discovered by the locals, they might never have come to our attention."

Kian turned over in his sleep and began to snore softly, his breath whistling between his tiny fangs.

"I don't get that part," said Luke. "Why would the locals take Kian's mom away like that?"

"Vampires are feared all over the world," replied Alston Negative. "If you live outside of a G.H.O.U.L. community, as Kian and his mother seem to have, you try to keep your identity under wraps for fear of attack."

"If they were keeping it secret, then how did people find out they were vampires?" asked Cleo.

Resus shrugged. "You've seen the kid in action and heard him announce that he's a vampire. I guess the wrong person must have overheard him and spread the word."

"Is there any chance his mom will come and find him?" said Luke.

"If he's telling the truth about her attackers' carrying wooden stakes, I don't think that's going to happen," answered Bella.

There was a soft knock on the door, and Mr. Watson entered. "There's still a handful of people from our world out there," he said. "I keep thinking I should be apologizing for their behavior."

Alston Negative stood and shook his neighbor's hand. "No apologies required," he said. "Just as there are rogue vampires, there are also

normals who don't live up to the best their kind can be."

"I suppose that's true," agreed Luke's dad. "You know me and Sue. We're normals, and we're both decent enough!" Resus and Cleo glanced at each other uncomfortably.

"Would you like a drink?" Bella asked.

Mr. Watson shook his head. "I can't stay. I've got to get back and try to design some sort of disguise for the Crudleys: they're determined not to be kept indoors again tomorrow." He turned to Luke. "Are you coming? Your mom should be home by now."

"Um, not just yet," replied Luke. "Resus, Cleo, and I are going to find Kian's grandpa and let him know where he is."

"Are we?" inquired Resus, which prompted a swift kick under the table from Luke. "*Ow!* I mean, er . . . we are! It would be a shame to wake the kid up, so I was hoping my mom would say he could stay the night."

"No sense disturbing him," agreed Cleo.

"And we don't want his grandpa to worry, so we'll stop by, introduce ourselves, and let him know that everything's OK," finished Luke.

  104

"Very considerate of you," said Mr. Watson. "I'll leave the back door unlocked so you don't disturb me and your mom when you come in. I think we'll be having an early night after today."

"Mom's staying at Eefa's tonight!" Luke blurted out.

"Is she?" asked Mr. Watson. "Why?"

"She, um . . . found all Dr. Skully's bones, but they need cleaning before they can be put back together," said Luke, trying not to catch the eye of anyone else in the room. "You know how messy normals can be!"

"I guess so. . . ." Luke's dad didn't sound convinced.

"So, Mum and Eefa are having a girly night, chatting about—you know—girly things, while they clean off the bones," Luke continued. "She told me to tell you she'd see you tomorrow."

Mr. Watson said nothing for a moment, then cleared his throat. "I can tell when you're lying to me, Luke."

Luke felt his cheeks redden. "What?" he said. "I'm not—"

"Tell me where your mom is."

"I didn't . . ." began Luke. "I mean . . ."

 105

Resus felt his friend squirm beside him. He glanced at Cleo and saw that the mummy was suddenly finding the bandage around her left knee very interesting.

"Tell me the truth!" insisted Mr. Watson.

"OK," sighed Luke. "Since your birthday's coming up, Mom's been planning something special with Eefa."

"OK, OK," said his dad quickly. "Don't say any more — and I won't let your mom know you caved in so easily." Pulling on his jacket, he added, "Just make sure you don't stay out too late — you never know what those normals will try next!" And with a chuckle, he left.

As soon as the door closed behind his dad, Luke jumped to his feet. "Come on," he said to Resus and Cleo. "We don't want to keep Kian's grandpa waiting."

"No, we don't," agreed Resus as Luke practically dragged him from the room. "Mom, Dad, see you later. I'll be back—"

The door slammed before he could finish the sentence.

Out in the street, the vampire rounded on Luke. "How long are you going to keep this up?"

 106

"I don't know what you're talking about," said Luke.

"You know exactly what I mean," barked the vampire. "You have to tell your dad that that werewolf in the square is really your mom."

"I can't do that!" cried Luke. "How do you think he'll feel when he finds out he's the only normal in Scream Street?"

"That's a bit of an understatement," said Cleo with a laugh, stepping into the shadows as a group of drunken tourists staggered past.

"OK, then, brainy bandages," Luke snapped. "The only normal *living* in Scream Street!"

"Apart from Resus and Sir Otto, you mean?" she asked.

Luke glared at her.

"Your dad will figure out what's happened sooner or later, Luke," said Resus. "And it'll only make him more upset when he finds out you've lied to him."

"Which house has Kian been moved into?" asked Luke, ignoring him. "We need to tell his grandpa where he is."

"Luke, you're not listening . . ." began Resus.

Cleo shook her head and frowned at the

vampire. "Apparently it's number thirty-one," she said. "That's next door to the Howls."

The trio had to cross the square to reach Kian's house, passing the blond werewolf, which lay curled up in its cage, whining softly. A few normals were still taking photographs, even at this late hour.

The windows of 31 Scream Street were dark. "Are you sure this is the right house?" Resus asked as he knocked on the front door. "It looks abandoned to me."

"This is definitely the one," confirmed Cleo. "Kian's wrist tag had thirty-one on it."

Resus knocked again, louder this time. "Well, either his grandpa's stone deaf or he's popped his cape and gone to the big blood bank in the sky."

"Don't say that!" said Cleo. "I'd hate to think of Kian being all alone."

Resus shrugged. "Either way, no one's answering the door."

"Can you pick the lock?" asked Luke.

"That's a great idea," retorted Resus. "We'll break in and then you can lie about that, too!" He pretended to be Luke. "No, Dad," he said innocently. "Of course we didn't go into the vampire's house without permission."

"You think this is funny?" growled Luke.

Cleo stepped between them. "No one thinks it's funny," she said, trying the door. "And no one needs to break in anywhere—it's unlocked." Resus stepped forward, but the mummy stopped him. "Either you two stop this right now or I'm going home."

"Stop what?" demanded Luke.

"Stop acting like a pair of . . . like a pair of boys!"

Luke sighed. "OK," he grunted.

"Fair enough," Resus mumbled.

"Go on," insisted Cleo. "Make friends!"

Reluctantly, Luke took Resus's hand and shook it. "Can we go in now?" he asked Cleo.

"Of course!" she exclaimed, opening the door wider.

"It's funny that this vampire, whoever he is, doesn't seem to be worried about his grandson," said Resus. "He's not exactly out searching the streets for Kian, is he? And it's the poor kid's first night here!"

"Try not to point out his lack of grand-parenting skills when we find him," Luke said with a grin, stepping into the dark hallway. He flicked a switch. "No lights."

"No problem!" said Resus, pulling a flaming torch from his cloak. The hallway was quickly illuminated. Cobwebs hung down from the ceiling, and spiders scuttled away from the visitors, leaving tracks in the thick dust that covered every surface.

"I see they've gone for the traditional haunted house theme," quipped Luke.

"Maybe it's to make Kian feel at home," suggested Cleo. "As if he's back in his castle with his mom."

"I doubt it," said Resus, running his finger over the surface of a table in the hall. "This isn't designer, decorative dust, it's the this-place-hasn't-been-cleaned-for-years stuff."

Luke peered into the kitchen. "Three faucets," he confirmed, pointing to the sink. "There *is* a vampire living here, after all." As neck-biting wasn't considered good neighborly behavior on Scream Street, vampires had their blood supply pumped directly into their homes—once the red blood had been filtered out of the rest of the world's wastewater supply.

"Well, he should get himself a housekeeper," declared Cleo. "Kian can't come and live with his grandpa in this mess!"

"Wherever this grandfather *is*," added Resus, "there's no sign of him down here."

"Then let's go up," said Luke, heading for the stairs.

The trio found the coffin in one of the bedrooms. The wood was aging and splintered, and it was also covered in dust and spiderwebs.

"Typical," groaned Cleo. "Wherever we go, there's always a coffin."

"Well, they're very comfy to sleep in," Resus said.

"It looks like Kian's grandpa might be sleeping in, then," quipped Luke. "I don't think this one's been opened for a while."

Resus wedged the flaming torch in the back of a broken chair. "Until now."

"I knew you were going to say that." Cleo sighed.

"Go on, then," Luke urged Resus. "He's *your* relative."

Gritting his fangs, Resus gripped the edge of the lid of the coffin and swung it up. The rusted hinges disintegrated with the effort, and the lid crashed to the floor, sending up a cloud of dust and dirt.

As the air cleared, the trio leaned forward to peer into the coffin.

It was empty.

Chapter Eleven
The Idea

"I told you there couldn't be any other vampires living in Scream Street," said Resus, as he, Luke, and Cleo stepped out of the house, brushing the dust off their clothes.

"Well, G.H.O.U.L. obviously thinks he's still here, or it would have relocated Kian somewhere else," said Cleo.

"That's true," Resus conceded. "And if there was anywhere better to send him, I don't think they'd be resorting to some anonymous grandfather. In a way, it's a good thing he kicked things off today, or he'd still be sitting in that horrible place now, all by himself."

"Yeah, but my mom wouldn't be locked in a cage like a circus sideshow," Luke pointed out.

"I didn't say it was all good news," said Resus, sliding the flaming torch back under his cloak.

"Meanwhile, what should we do about Kian?" asked Cleo.

"I'm sure my mom and dad will let him stay at our house for the time being," replied Resus. "He *is* family, after all." He yawned and stretched. "I'd better go and let them know what we found—or didn't find—at his grandpa's house."

"I'm going to stay with my mom tonight," said Luke.

Resus looked surprised. "Outside? In the square?"

Luke nodded. "Could you pop a note through my door to tell my dad I'm sleeping at your house?"

"I'm not getting involved in this lie," Resus said.

"You're not," insisted Luke. "If he finds out, I'll tell him it was all me. I just don't want my mom to be alone."

"OK," said Resus shortly. And without another word, he set off for home.

"I should get back, too," said Cleo, "or my dad will be wondering where I've gone. Are you going to be OK?"

Luke, staring after Resus, didn't reply.

"Luke," said Cleo, shaking him gently on the arm, "will you be OK?"

"I'll be fine," he assured her. "I'm just finding it hard having Resus tell me what I should and shouldn't say to my dad."

"Don't worry about him," said Cleo reassuringly. "He's just a bit thrown about Kian, that's all. He'll be back to his usual self tomorrow."

Luke gave a half smile. "Can't wait," he said. "'Night."

He watched Cleo disappear into the darkness, then headed back to his mom's cage. The square was almost deserted now; the only other person in sight was Dixon. The landlord's nephew sat on a stool next to the shimmering doorway, clutching the money bag, his head bobbing as he struggled

to fight off sleep. Sir Otto had probably put him on night duty in case a horde of nocturnal normals arrived.

The blond werewolf sniffed the air as Luke approached the cage. "Hi, Mom," Luke said softly. "I thought I'd come and see how you were doing." The wolf settled its head back onto its paws.

Luke pulled *The G.H.O.U.L. Guide* from his pocket and sat down beside the cage. "Why isn't she changing back, Mr. Skipstone?" he asked.

"Your mother's wolf stayed dormant within her for a very long time," replied the author, his golden face glinting in the moonlight. "Much longer than it does for most of us. It could be a while before she transforms back, Luke, but you mustn't lose hope. Your mom *will* come back to you."

"Yeah." Luke sighed. "That's exactly what we told Kian."

And, with a final glance at the cage, he curled up on the cold, hard concrete and went to sleep beside his mom.

Crash! Luke was woken just after dawn. Dixon, having finally surrendered to sleep, had fallen off his stool and landed face-first on the ground. The money bag had burst open, spilling bills and coins everywhere.

Luke rubbed his eyes and looked around him. His mom's werewolf was pacing around the cage, growling.

"You moron!" screamed a voice. Sir Otto

Sneer was racing across the square, still in his pajamas and slippers. "Dixon!" yelled the landlord, dropping to his knees and gathering the spilled money back up into the leather bag. "Wake up!"

His nephew raised his head with a tired groan, two coins jammed into his eye sockets. He pulled them free and stood, dazed. Raising his hand in a halfhearted attempt to wave at Luke, he slurred:

"Shall I compare thee to a summer's day?
Thou art more lovely, and have fewer wasps!"

Sir Otto slapped his nephew across the back of the head, dislodging a third coin from Dixon's left nostril. "Stop that nonsense and help me catch my money!"

Staggering dizzily, Dixon joined in the chase as bills were picked up by the breeze and blown in circles around the square. The landlord jumped and grasped frantically at the fluttering money.

"I'll help," called Luke. "In return for the key to my mom's cage."

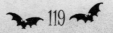

Sir Otto spun to face him. "Nice try, freak, but your mother is worth more to me than a few missing dollars. Come back when you really have something to bargain with."

Then Luke had an idea. . .

"You want us to do *what*?" demanded Resus.

The trio was sitting in Cleo's bedroom. Luke had come over to enlist the support of the mummy and had found Resus already there.

"You want us to steal Sir Otto's money?"

"We're not going to *keep* it," insisted Luke. "We'll just hold on to it until he swaps it for the key to my mom's cage."

"I'm still not sure," said Resus. "I know we have taken relics in the past, but they were left behind on purpose for someone to find and use."

"We broke into Sneer's house when I first moved here, to get *Skipstone's Tales of Scream Street*," Luke reminded him.

"I like to think of that as more of a rescue than a theft," countered Resus. "Sir Otto had kidnapped Mr. Skipstone—if you *can* kidnap a person who's mostly a book, that is. We didn't just go in there to take stuff."

"I've *told* you," said Luke. "We won't keep the money. He can have it back once he's given me the key."

"But we agreed you couldn't just set your mom free in her current state," said Cleo. "She could end up hurting someone, or worse."

"OK," agreed Luke. "We'll tell him he has to give us the cage as well. We can set it up in my backyard. Mr. Skipstone says my mom will transform back at some point. She'll just have to live behind bars until she does."

"If you do that, there's no way you'll be able to hide her condition from your dad," said Resus.

"But that might be for the best," added Cleo.

Luke sighed. "I know."

"So, you'll tell him the truth?" she asked.

Luke grinned. "If it'll get you two off my back."

"I'm still not happy about stealing Sneer's money," said Resus.

"We need a bargaining tool to help my mom," Luke explained, "and what better than the contents of Sir Otto's pockets?"

"You know he'll just make more by continuing

to charge normals to come to Scream Street, don't you?" said Cleo.

"Probably," replied Luke, "but you should have seen him this morning, scrabbling around in his pajamas to save his precious cash. He won't give up what he's already earned without a fight."

"All right," agreed Resus. "I don't like it, but I'll do it."

"Awesome!" said Luke, delighted.

"After Luke has spoken to his dad, of course," added Cleo.

The square was packed with normals again by the time Luke, Resus, and Cleo left the house. Sir Otto was back at the doorway, stuffing money into his pouch as more and more tourists flooded through.

"This way, thrill-seeking ladies and gentlemen!" he bellowed. "Just two hundred dollars each to enter the freakiest street in the world. Witness the werewolves, see the skeletons, visit the vampires!"

The other residents were generally nowhere to be seen—although Twinkle was out with Scapula, searching for the missing pieces of Dr.

Skully. Whenever the dog picked up his master's scent on one of the normals, the hefty fairy asked the person in question to hand over the bone. No one, so far, had refused.

Dixon was back at his makeshift poetry post, loudly performing rhymes—although no one was paying the slightest bit of attention:

> "Peter is a furry worm
> Who lives inside a bush.
> I hit him with a concrete slab,
> Now Peter's furry mush!

"Maybe he should team up with Mr. Skipstone," Cleo said with a laugh. "They could bring out a book of pathetic poetry togeth—"

She stopped.

"What is it?" asked Luke, following her gaze. The crowd around the werewolf's cage shifted slightly, and he saw what Cleo was looking at— his dad, standing beside the cage, staring sadly at the creature inside.

"Dad!" he called, hurrying over.

Mr. Watson didn't look up. "You knew, didn't you?"

Luke reddened. "It wasn't like that . . ."

"*Didn't you?*"

Luke was silent for a moment. "Yes," he said quietly.

"Why didn't you tell me?" asked Mr. Watson, turning to his son. "Why lie about something as big as this?"

"I didn't think you'd . . ." Luke's words trailed off.

"What?" snapped his dad. "Be able to cope?"

"Something like that," Luke admitted.

"You wouldn't believe the things your mom and I have had to cope with since you became who you are!" cried Mr. Watson. "It wasn't easy, but we always did it—together. Only this time, you kept us apart."

"I—I'm sorry."

Mr. Watson looked back at the werewolf.

"We should take her home."

"Sneer won't let us move her," said Luke.

"He will by the time I've finished with him!" declared Mr. Watson, setting off in the direction of the landlord.

Luke grabbed his dad's arm to stop him. "Let me do it," he said. Mr. Watson turned to look at him. "I was the one who caused her transformation, and I was the one who hid it from you. Give me a chance to fix things."

"And if you can't?"

"We'll rope off the corner of the square and you can fight it out with Sir Otto yourself," Luke said with a smile.

Mr. Watson looked intently into his son's eyes. "Bring your mom home," he said.

Luke nodded. "I will, Dad. I promise."

With a final sad glance at the werewolf, Mr. Watson walked away. Resus and Cleo came over to their friend.

"Are you OK?" asked Cleo.

"I will be once we get my mom out of all this." Luke sighed. "Come on."

Resus and Cleo followed him toward the gates to Sneer Hall. Thankfully, the crowds blocked Sir Otto's view, and the landlord was unable to see the trio slip inside and dash across the lawn.

"I hope Sneer hasn't got his hellhounds patrolling the grounds," said Cleo as they made their way from the cover of a tree to a nearby clump of bushes.

"I doubt it," said Resus. "He doesn't want

another hungry monster on the loose! Sorry," he added, catching Luke's expression.

When they reached the house, they pressed themselves up against one of its huge walls and slid round to the door they knew led to the massive kitchen inside.

"This is nail-biting stuff!" joked Resus, pulling off one of his fake vampire talons and slipping it into the lock. The false nails were as strong as steel, and Resus had used them many times before to gain entry to locked buildings. He twisted the nail, and . . . *snap!*

"What's wrong?" asked Luke.

"It broke," groaned Resus.

"Broke?" said Luke. "I thought those things were invincible!"

"Not against titanium locks," replied Resus, crouching to examine the door. "It looks like Sneer's upgraded his security."

"What do we do now?" asked Cleo.

"We could try another door," suggested Resus.

Luke shook his head. "If he's changed one lock, he'll have changed them all."

"There's a window open up there," said Cleo, pointing to the top floor.

"We'll never get up there without a ladder," Luke said with a sigh.

"Then we need to think of something else," said Resus. "Any ideas?"

"I'm a vampire!" announced a voice.

Chapter Twelve
The Raid

"Kian!" hissed Resus, pulling the small vampire flat against the wall beside him. "What are you doing here?"

"Your mom told me you went to see my grandpa last night," the boy said, beaming. "Did he say when I can meet him?"

"He, uh . . . wasn't in," said Resus. "But we're going to look for him again later."

"Is he in there?" asked Kian, pointing at the mansion.

"No, he's not in there," replied Cleo. "And you shouldn't be here, either—you could get into trouble!"

Kian didn't falter. "Why?"

"Because we're . . . we're . . ." Cleo shrugged. "Luke?"

"Because we can't let anyone know we're here," Luke explained.

"Why?"

"Because some people wouldn't be happy if they knew what we were doing."

"Why?"

Luke bit back an impatient retort. "Because . . . Because it's a secret!"

"Like a secret mission?" asked Kian.

"That's it," agreed Resus. "We're on a top-secret mission."

"Can I come, too?" asked Kian excitedly. "I'm really good at keeping secrets. I'm a vampire!"

The trio exchanged worried looks. "He can't

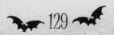

come inside Sneer Hall with us," whispered Luke. "Anything could happen!"

"Well, we can't send him back by himself," Cleo pointed out. "Someone might spot him and want to know what he's doing here."

"To be honest, I can't see us getting inside at all," said Resus. "If all the locks are titanium, my nails won't work on any of them."

"I could change into a bat and fly up to that open window, go inside, come downstairs, and open the door for you," suggested Kian. "You can get in that way."

Luke, Resus, and Cleo stared at the boy in silence for a few seconds.

"You've got yourself a mission!" exclaimed Luke. "But be careful in there."

"I'm always careful," said Kian with a grin. "I'm a vampire!"

The boy spun round swiftly and changed into a bat amid a cloud of black smoke. Flapping its wings, the bat rose into the air and slipped through the open window.

"OK," said Luke. "Let's get to the door so we're ready for him."

"Which one?" asked Cleo.

"What?"

"Which door is Kian going to open?"

Luke felt his cheeks redden. "I, er . . . I don't know."

"What do you mean, you don't know?" demanded Resus.

"I didn't tell him which door to open," admitted Luke. "But you didn't, either!" he added defensively.

"He could be anywhere in there by now," cried Resus. "That place is huge."

"I'm sure he won't get lost," said Cleo.

"Of course he'll get lost!" exclaimed Resus. "He's just a little kid, and Sneer Hall is like a maze. In fact, I'll be surprised if we ever—"

Click! The door closest to the trio swung open and Kian appeared, grinning out at them.

"Can we start the secret mission now?" he whispered.

Luke, Resus, Cleo, and Kian crept up the nearest staircase and into Sir Otto Sneer's second-floor study. Apart from the small group of trespassers, the mansion appeared to be deserted—and thankfully the landlord's hellhounds were nowhere to be seen.

"If Sneer's keeping the money anywhere, it'll be in his safe," said Luke.

"What safe?" asked Cleo, looking around the room. Aside from dozens of well-stocked book-shelves, the only furniture was a desk, a leather chair and a slightly moth-eaten sofa.

Luke shrugged. "My guess is, he'll have one hidden behind a painting or in a secret compart-ment in one of the bookshelves," he said.

"Meaning it will take forever to find," Cleo said, sighing.

"Not necessarily," said Resus. "Safes are, invariably, made from metal—so all we need is something that's attracted to the stuff."

"Goblins!" exclaimed Cleo. "They're like magpies when it comes to shiny things. They'd be able to find a metal safe within minutes."

"Probably," agreed Resus. He patted his pockets. "But I appear to be all out of goblins at the moment. . . . I do, however, have this!" He pulled a metal detector from the folds of his cloak and switched it on.

Kian gasped in excitement. "Does your cape do that, too?" he squeaked. "I've got all sorts of stuff in here!" He began to pull an assortment of items from his own cloak. "I've got a stapler, a radio, a cookbook, a rubber chicken . . ."

While Kian was busy emptying out his cape, Resus slipped on a pair of headphones and began to run the metal detector along the rows of books. Luke and Cleo, meanwhile, checked behind the many paintings that hung on the study walls.

"A newspaper, a bottle opener, a spinning wheel, a rosebush . . ."

"Nothing behind there," said Luke when he and Cleo had finished. "Maybe it's sunk into the floor somewhere." Dropping to their knees, the pair began to run their fingers over the thick carpet.

"A hatstand, a pair of scissors, a cookie, a baby's rattle . . ."

Beep, beep! Resus pulled a handful of books off one of the shelves to reveal a small silver door behind. "Got it!"

Luke and Cleo hurried over, and even Kian stopped taking inventory of his belongings to peer at the safe, buried deep in the wall.

Luke pulled at the wheel-like handle. "It's locked," he said.

"You don't say," observed Resus sarcastically.

"But it's got one of those combination things," continued Luke.

"Except we don't have the combination," said Cleo.

"I read a book once where some bank robbers used a doctor's stethoscope to listen for the clicks as they turned the wheel," Luke told them. He

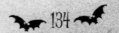

looked at Resus and Kian. "Either of you got a stethoscope in your capes?"

Resus had a quick rummage around inside his. "No, sorry," he said.

"I've got a toy cow," said Kian. "Does that help? I've also got a stepladder, a grapefruit, a boomerang, a teapot . . ."

"It's OK," Luke assured him quickly. "I'll just have to do this the old-fashioned way."

He closed his eyes and pictured his mom's werewolf locked in the cage in the square, a crowd of normals leering and taking photographs. Photographs that would bring even more gawking tourists to Scream Street.

Anger bubbled inside Luke's mind, and he pictured it as a black liquid, spreading out across his face. Within seconds, his ears began to stretch out and rise to the top of his head.

Kian giggled. "You look like a gnome!"

The partial transformation now complete, Luke pressed his ears against the cold metal door of the safe and began to slowly turn the wheel. Each tiny click was amplified a hundred times to his werewolf senses, and he was easily able to hear the difference between the noise of the

wheel turning and the almost silent sound of the safe's bolts sliding open.

"Twelve to the right," Luke said to himself. "Eighteen to the left. Nine to the right. Twenty-two to the left, and . . ." With a soft hiss, the vacuum seal around the edge of the door released as the safe unlocked.

"Amazing!" said Cleo. "If you ever decide to join Sneer instead of battling him, there's a career as a safe-cracker waiting for you!"

"I'd rather be a cook for Doug, Turf, and Berry," Luke said with a grin. He reached out to open the safe door. Resus stopped him.

"I don't like this," he said. "No matter what we call it, it's still stealing."

Luke sighed as his ears returned to normal. "It's not stealing if we don't keep it for ourselves," he insisted. "All Sneer has to do is hand my mom over, then he can have his dirty money right back."

"I don't know. . . ."

"Look," said Luke, finally opening the door. "You don't have to be involved in this at all. *I* was the one who came up with this idea,

I was the one who broke into the safe, and *I'll* be the one to take the money."

"What money?" asked Kian.

The trio stared. The little vampire was right: the safe was completely empty.

"If there's nothing in there to steal," said Resus, "why do I still feel like we're a bunch of thieves?"

"Because you *are* a bunch of thieves!" roared the voice of Sir Otto behind them.

Chapter Thirteen
The Poem

"Well, I've finally caught you stealing from me," growled Sneer. "I'll see that G.H.O.U.L. sends you to the Underlands for this."

"We haven't stolen anything!" exclaimed Luke. "The safe was already empty when we opened it."

"Maybe it was, maybe it wasn't," said the landlord. "But I know which story I'll be passing on to Zeal Chillchase—"

"Are you my grandpa?" interrupted Kian.

"What?" barked Sir Otto.

"I'm looking for my grandpa," explained Kian, unfazed by Sir Otto's glare. "He's a vampire. Are you him?"

"Get this little brat away from me!" bellowed Sneer. "How *dare* he accuse me of being a freak like the rest of you?"

Resus hurried over to Kian and quickly ushered him away. "He's not your grandpa," he explained. "He's a very nasty man."

"*I'm* the nasty one, am I?" Sneer laughed. "May I point out that I'm not the one who's just been caught breaking into a locked safe?"

"We were only trying to help Luke's mom," protested Cleo. "You're the one who locked her up!"

"And all for a worthy cause," said Sir Otto, smirking. "Me! She is, after all, my biggest attraction." He shook his leather money bag to illustrate his point.

"Until she transforms back, that is," said

Resus. "After that, who's going to pay to see a woman locked in a cage?"

"Normals will pay," declared Sneer, dropping the bag onto his desk. "Normals who will anger her night and day with their insults and their camera flashes. If they happen to see her transform in person, I'll charge them extra for the privilege. Who knows, I might even make them pay to watch feeding time."

"You can't do that!" cried Cleo.

"Just watch me."

Luke clenched his fists, but Resus shook his head. "He's not worth it," he said.

"Oh, but I *am* worth it," countered Sir Otto. "For when the normals tire of the werewolf, I'll put *your* parents in the cage, boy! A few days without their precious blood supply, and those pathetic vampires will be biting anything I throw at them."

"I'll kill you!" roared Resus, racing for the landlord. Sir Otto knocked the vampire aside with a swipe of his hand, sending him crashing into the pile of objects Kian had produced from his cape. The items fell on top of Sir Otto's money bag and, one after the other, disappeared inside it.

"It works just like a vampire's cape!" exclaimed Kian.

"You idiots!" shouted Sneer as he snatched up the bag and peered inside. "You've pushed all the money down to the bottom!" He stormed toward the door. "I'll be back once I've contacted Chillchase."

And in a flash, the landlord had slammed the door behind him and turned the key, locking the children inside his study.

"Is that man angry with me?" asked Kian.

"He's angry with everyone," said Cleo kindly. "Don't let him worry you."

"But how will we find my grandpa if we're locked in here?"

"We'll find a way," Resus reassured him. "I don't quite know how, but we will."

"At least we now know where Sneer's been keeping his money," said Luke, slumping into the armchair. "It's all inside that leather bag."

"It was just like my vampire's cape," Kian said again.

"It's probably got the same sort of spell on it," said Resus. "Typical Sneer—he doesn't trust anyone, so he carries his cash with him everywhere he goes."

"The only chance I had of making him release my mom, and I can't get anywhere near it," sighed Luke.

There was a timid tap on the door.

"Who's there?" asked Cleo.

"Dixon," came the reply. "Uncle Otto says I have to come up here and stand guard, and that while I'm at it, I should tell you some of my horrible poetry."

"Wonderful," Resus said, groaning.

Dixon cleared his throat and began, very quietly, to recite his latest composition so that it could just be heard through the door:

> "My uncle says my poems stink,
> It makes me very sad.
> And so I'm going to do something
> That's bound to make him mad.
>
> If you want to make him cross,
> To tear out all his hair,
> Take a look at what you find
> Right beneath his . . ."

"That's the worst so far," muttered Luke.

"It doesn't even rhyme," agreed Resus.

Cleo hurried over to the door. "Dixon," she called, pressing her face to the wood. "Say that last verse again!"

"No, don't," moaned Resus. "Isn't it bad enough to be trapped in here, without having to endure this torture from the rotten rhymer?"

"*Shh!*" hissed Cleo. "Dixon, please tell it to me again."

"Why do you want . . . ?" began Luke.

Cleo glared at him. "Because it's a clue, dummy. Now—get over here and listen!"

Luke dashed to the door. "OK, Dixon," he called. "Tell us your poem again—one more time, please."

"Just remember that you worked it out for yourselves," whined Dixon. "I didn't tell you anything!"

"We won't say a word," promised Resus.

Dixon whispered the entire rhyme a second time:

> "My uncle says my poems stink,
>   It makes me very sad.
> And so I'm going to do something
>   That's bound to make him mad.

 143

If you want to make him cross,
To tear out all his hair,
Take a look at what you find
Right beneath his . . ."

Luke stepped back from the door and looked around the room. "Right beneath his . . . *bear?*" He shrugged. "Has Sir Otto got a bearskin in here?"

"Not that I can see," answered Resus. "What about *pair?*"

"Pair of what?" asked Cleo.

"I dunno."

Luke paced about, listing words at random. "Flare . . . mare . . . dare . . . lair . . . chair . . ." His eyes lit up. *"Chair!"* He dropped to his knees and slid Sir Otto's chair away from his desk to examine the carpet beneath. "Nothing." He sighed.

"Try looking under the carpet," suggested Resus.

Gripping the edge of the carpet at the wall, Luke and Cleo rolled it back as far as Sir Otto's chair to reveal a small hatch in the floorboards.

"A trapdoor!" exclaimed the mummy.

Luke pulled open the small door and peered

into the darkness. "Yes, but where does it lead?" he asked.

"Anywhere's better than here," replied Resus.

"Not if we get stuck underneath the floor-boards," Cleo pointed out.

Resus produced his flaming torch, but Luke shook his head. "I wouldn't take that down

there," he said. "The floor could ignite and burn us all to a crisp."

"I've got a light," announced Kian, pulling a flashlight from his own cape and handing it to Luke. Resus put the flame away.

"There's a ladder!" cried Luke, as the torch began to pierce the gloom. "This must be some sort of escape hatch."

"Then what are we waiting for?" Resus said with a grin.

Luke climbed into the hole first, tapping each rung of the ladder with his foot to test its strength before placing his entire weight on it. Step by step, he gradually disappeared into the darkness. Kian went next, closely followed by Resus. As Cleo brought up the rear, she called out, "Dixon, I could kiss you!"

As the hatch closed behind them, there was a moment of silence before, on the other side of the locked door, Dixon gave a happy sigh.

Chapter Fourteen
The Escape

At the bottom of the ladder, the hole became a tunnel that seemed to slope down from the second-floor study and then run between the walls on the first floor. Gripping Kian's flashlight between his teeth, Luke led the way along the low, dirty passageway on his hands and knees.

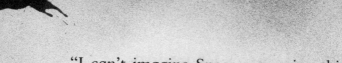

"I can't imagine Sneer ever using this as an escape route," said Resus as he, Kian, and Cleo followed Luke through the dusty tunnel. "There's no way he'd ever fit down here!"

"I can fit," said Kian, who was clearly having a great time. "I'm a vampire."

"Well, I hope you've got a fresh set of bandages in your cloak," Cleo said, laughing. "These ones are getting ruined!"

After a few minutes, Luke came to a stop.

"What's the matter?" asked Resus.

"The tunnel splits in two," replied Luke. "Do we go left or right? The last thing we want is to come out in another locked room somewhere."

"It depends on where we are now," said Cleo. "I have no idea, I'm afraid."

"I'm completely lost," admitted Resus.

"Well, I'm pretty sure the study is more or less above Sneer's dining room," said Luke thoughtfully. "Which *should* mean the tunnel on the right goes deeper into the house, while the left one heads toward the outside wall . . ."

"And freedom!" pronounced Resus.

"Left it is, then," said Cleo.

Luke turned and crawled along the left-hand

passageway, the others following close behind. Before long, he could feel cool air on his face. "I think we're getting close to an exit," he called over his shoulder.

"There's a shaft of light up ahead," said Resus, peering past his friend.

The light was seeping around the edges of a small door set into the wall of the tunnel. By edging past it slightly, Luke was able to push his foot out and kick open the wooden flap. Daylight streamed into the tunnel.

"He shoots. He scores!" Resus cried as Luke scrambled back to peer out of the opening.

"It's not much of a drop down," he told them. "Ten feet or so." He slid his legs out of the door and disappeared from view. "Hand Kian down to me," he called back.

Resus lowered the younger vampire out of the tunnel, then he and Cleo jumped down themselves. They seemed to be in some kind of small, high-walled courtyard.

"I'd say that was some pretty good navigating," boasted Luke, but before anyone could reply, a pair of deep-throated growls made them spin around. Sir Otto's two vicious hellhounds

were slinking across the courtyard toward the small group, fire flashing in their eyes and acidic saliva dripping from their jaws.

"Yeah," agreed Cleo sarcastically. "If we'd been unlucky, we could have ended up in another locked room!"

"I wondered where Sneer had been keeping these two," murmured Resus.

"Well, now you know," answered Luke, his eyes scanning the high walls around them for an escape route.

"Nice doggies," said Kian, beaming. He stepped toward the snarling pair.

"NO!" cried Luke, Resus, and Cleo together, grabbing the boy and pulling him back.

"You don't want to pet one of those," exclaimed Cleo. "Or you'll find yourself missing a few fingers!"

"Not if I don't have any to start with," declared Kian. Spinning himself around, he swiftly transformed into a bat and flapped off across the courtyard. Transfixed, the hellhounds followed, leaping into the air and barking angrily.

"He's distracting them so we can escape!" cried Luke in amazement.

Resus grinned. "I could get used to having him around," he said.

"We still have to get over the wall," Cleo reminded them.

"Sounds like a job for me," said Resus, reaching into his cloak and pulling out a length of rope with a metal grappling hook at one end. As Kian continued to divert the hellhounds by flitting around above them, Resus threw the hook up and over the wall, where it wedged securely.

Cleo climbed up first, with Luke and Resus pushing from behind to hurry her along. From the top of the wall, the mummy reached down and helped Luke to clamber up beside her. Last, Resus joined them.

"OK, Kian," called Luke. "We're ready to go now!" But instead of flapping over to join them, Kian changed back into a boy right where he was.

"I'm a really useful vampire," he exclaimed.

Cleo screamed. "Kian, *no!* Change back— quickly!"

It was too late. The hellhounds were on him in a second, snapping and growling as the small vampire tried to cover his face with his hands.

Luke, Resus, and Cleo leaped down from the wall and raced back across the courtyard, the vampire pulling out his flaming torch as he ran. He thrust the flame between Kian and the snarling dogs, causing them to yelp in pain and pull away.

Cleo dived beneath the torch and grabbed the small vampire, dragging him clear. "I've got him!" she called.

Resus lunged forward again with the torch as the enraged creatures turned to follow their prey, but the fire wouldn't hold them back for long. "Get him over the wall," Resus instructed Cleo. "Luke and I will see to these things!"

"How exactly are we going to do that?" Luke asked him as Cleo and Kian ran for the rope and began to climb up it.

"Reach inside my cloak," replied Resus calmly. "Grab the first thing you can find—then clobber them with it!"

Sliding his hand into the silky lining of the vampire's cape, Luke grasped what felt like a metal handle. "I've got something!"

"What?"

"Only one way to find out!" Luke pulled his arm out and found himself gripping the handle of a frying pan. "Perfect!" he cried, swinging

 153

the pan around and catching the first hellhound on the side of the head, knocking it out cold. Its companion leaped for Luke, teeth gnashing, only to receive a kick from Resus that sent it sprawling. By the time it was back on its feet, Luke had brought the frying pan down on its head with a satisfying *clunk*!

Luke tossed the pan to the ground; the dogs' caustic drool was already beginning to eat into the thick metal. "Not bad," he said, panting.

Resus swung the flaming torch round and slipped it back into his cape like a cowboy holstering a six-shooter. "Out of the fire and into the frying pan!" he quipped.

The boys then clambered quickly up the rope and dropped down on the other side of the wall, finding themselves at the opposite side of Sneer Hall from the square. Cleo was waiting for them, alone.

"Where's Kian?" asked Luke.

Cleo looked around her in surprise. "He was here a minute ago!"

"It's like babysitting a poltergeist," said Resus in exasperation. "We'll have to find him. He's a magnet for trouble when he's by himself."

"We'd better keep out of Sneer's way, though," said Luke. "As far as he's concerned, we're still locked in his study."

The trio crossed the yard and let themselves out of the gates, then stepped into the crowd of normals that filled the square. There were still plenty of people packed around the werewolf's cage, plus a group of boys lurching along after Doug.

The zombie seemed to have managed to sew his legs back in place, but he'd reattached them the wrong way around, so he faced his pursuers as he staggered away from them. "Dudes!" he complained. "Give a brother a little space, man."

The teenagers burst into laughter and continued to mock the zombie's swagger. "Space, man," drawled one of them.

Resus scowled as he watched Doug trying to escape. "He'd eat their brains," he said. "Only there wouldn't be enough to keep him going till dinner!"

"Any sign of Kian?" asked Cleo.

"I can't see him," said Luke, scanning the crowd.

"Let's try the emporium," suggested Resus.

Sticking to the more densely populated parts of the square, the trio managed to hide themselves among the normals as they made their way over to Everwell's Emporium. As they entered the shop, they found Eefa there, carefully removing the parrot costume from the bat who lived above the door.

"Have you seen Kian anywhere?" Luke asked her.

"Right behind you," replied Eefa, pointing back outside.

Luke turned to see the small vampire approaching them, his mouth split into a wide grin and Sir Otto's leather money bag clutched in his hand.

"Kian!" exclaimed Luke. He, Resus, and Cleo dashed back through the doors and ran toward him. "What are you doing with that?"

Kian cheerfully handed the bag over to Luke. "Now you can use the money to save your mom," he said.

Luke was at a loss for words. "I . . . I didn't mean . . ."

"WHERE'S MY MONEY?" roared a voice from the other side of the square. There was sudden silence, and the crowd of normals parted just enough for Sir Otto to catch sight of Luke holding the stolen money bag.

"You've done it now, Watson," bellowed the landlord. He pushed his way through the crowds to the cage, unlocked the door, and swung it wide open. "Get the boy, and I'll grant you your freedom!" he snarled to the werewolf inside.

Chapter Fifteen
The
Answer

The werewolf seemed to understand Sir
Otto's command perfectly. It leaped from the
cage and sprinted directly for Luke. The normals
screamed and ran, fighting to get as far as possible
from the snarling creature.

"Inside, quick!" Luke yelled to his friends, grabbing Kian by the cape and dragging him into the emporium. He and Resus slammed the doors and pressed their weight against them while Cleo led the small vampire to the relative safety of the storeroom.

Mrs. Watson's werewolf flung itself at the shop doors, rattling the glass and making Luke and Resus jump. Outside, there was a stampede as the square cleared.

"What do we do now?" said Luke as the wolf hurled itself angrily at the doors a second time.

"Eefa, can you cast a shield spell around the emporium?" asked Resus.

The witch shook her head. "Not without trapping the werewolf inside it with the rest of us," she replied. "It's too close!"

"Why's it coming for *us*?" asked Cleo, peering cautiously around the door of the storeroom

"It must be me!" cried Luke as the doors shook for a third time, almost knocking the boys off their feet. "My mom was going to attack me yesterday before you caught her. She must still have my scent in her—"

CRASH! Finally giving up on the doors, the

 159

blond werewolf launched itself at the shop window and leaped right through. Its claws skidded on the smooth, polished floor as it landed, sending it crashing into Eefa and knocking over a display unit. With burning eyes, the wolf spun to face Luke and began slowly to advance.

"What do I do?" he yelled.

"You'll have to transform," replied Resus, backing away. "Transform and stop it from hurting anyone."

"But . . . it's my mom!" exclaimed Luke.

"You've got no choice."

"I can't hurt her!"

"Do it!"

Shaking, Luke forced his eyes closed and attempted to picture a scene that would trigger his rage. He tried to recall the moment when Sir Otto had locked them in the study, but the image evaporated. Concentrating harder, he thought back to when Kian had disappeared beneath the rabid hellhounds—but again, the scene shattered and wouldn't stay with him.

Now Luke could feel the wolf's breath on his face, and he opened his eyes to see it looking right at him.

 160

"What are you waiting for?" cried Resus.

"I—I can't get angry," said Luke fearfully. "I'm too scared!"

His mom's werewolf raised its head and howled. The sound filled the shop, echoing crazily around Luke's head, and briefly he wondered why the last thing he would ever hear couldn't be something more pleasant.

The werewolf bared its fangs . . . and pounced.

Just at that moment, a figure leaped through the broken window and pushed Luke to the ground, taking the full force of the werewolf's attack. Luke scrambled to his feet and was horrified to see his dad thrashing about on the floor beneath the angry creature.

"Susan!" screamed Mr. Watson. "You have to stop this!"

The werewolf clamped its jaws around Mr. Watson's neck. Luke wanted to look away, but he couldn't move a single muscle. Was he really going to watch his mother murder his father, right in front of his eyes?

Suddenly, the wolf froze. Its muscles began to shudder, and the dark-blond fur began to disappear, shrinking back underneath the beast's

thick, leathery skin. Bones cracked and reshaped as Mrs. Watson began to transform back.

Luke sank to the floor, exhausted, and watched as his mom's face became recognizable once more. In less than a minute, Mr. Watson was holding his trembling, sobbing wife.

"It's OK," he whispered, stroking her hair. "It's OK. I'm here. It's all over."

Luke scrambled across the broken glass to his parents. "I thought . . . I thought you were going to . . ."

Luke's mom lifted her head, and resting her hand on his cheek she gazed into her son's eyes. "I'm so sorry!" she said, weeping.

Silence enveloped the emporium as everyone tried to catch their breath. Then suddenly a voice cried out, "Please, no!" It was Eefa Everwell.

Cleo hurried over to where Eefa was trying to lift a damaged display unit from the floor. The mummy leaned her weight to the effort, and between them they managed to shift it. Beneath, lying perfectly still, was the emporium's bat.

Eefa buried her head in Cleo's shoulder and began to cry. "He's been with me ever since I first came to live here," she wailed.

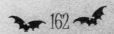

The sound of glass crunching under heavy boots caused Luke to look up to see Sir Otto Sneer standing over him. "Pathetic," the landlord said with a grunt, biting down on his cigar. "I can't even trust you freaks to kill each other properly."

Luke turned to glare at him.

"Well, come on, then," jeered Sir Otto. "Change into your little doggy thing and bite me: I might just have a surprise of my own."

"Resus is right," Luke muttered. "You're *not* worth it."

"You're all as bad as each other!" roared Sneer, stomping over the debris and the lifeless bat to reach his discarded money bag. "You're all monsters, fiends, oddities . . ." He turned to face Luke again. "And thieves!" With a final glance at Luke, the landlord stepped back through the broken window and strode off across the square.

One by one, the normals began to emerge from their hiding places, looking at the carnage in astonishment.

"Luke didn't steal your money!" called Kian, rushing out of the storeroom and pulling open the shop doors. "I did!"

The landlord turned back, then bent to study

the young boy, blowing a cloud of foul-smelling cigar smoke into his face. "You again," he growled. "I thought I knew all the freaks around here, but you're a new one. Just who *are* you?"

"I'm a vampire!" yelled Kian. And with that, he opened his mouth wide, sank his tiny fangs into the leather of Sir Otto's money bag, and tore it open. With the storage spell now broken, hundreds and thousands of dollars poured out of the bag and onto the ground. A cheer rose up from the normals as they fought to gather it up.

Sir Otto scrambled about among them, pushing people aside in a desperate effort to save his money, but the cash quickly disappeared into the pockets of the tourists. Eventually he gave up and turned his attention back to the small vampire.

"I'll make you pay!" he roared, raising his fist.

"You will not!" shouted an unfamiliar voice. Sir Otto looked up, startled. He squinted in the direction of Everwell's Emporium to establish who had spoken.

"Look!" hissed Cleo, pointing to where Eefa's bat had lain. A cloud of black smoke had gathered above it, and in a burst of light, an elderly vampire

had suddenly appeared in its place, his eyes pure white.

"You will not harm my grandson," warned the vampire as he walked slowly out of the shop.

"Grandad!" squealed Kian, racing over to the old man and flinging his arms around him. "It's me—Kian!"

The older vampire smiled. "I suspected it might be you," he said. "Unfortunately, I have spent so much time as a bat that I do not know if my sight will return. I fear I might never be able to set eyes upon you, my boy."

"I'll look after you," Kian promised, tucking his arm into his grandfather's. "I'm a vampire!"

The old man laughed. "I suspect, however, that I will always be able to *hear* you."

"This is all very touching," barked Sir Otto, "but it doesn't replace the money I'm owed."

The elderly vampire fixed his unseeing eyes upon Sneer. "I am Tarlo Negative," he declared. "Descended from one of Scream Street's founding fathers. If he could see what you have done to the lives of those he wished to protect, you would not live to see another dawn."

"B–But, my money . . ." moaned Sir Otto.

Tarlo continued to stare at the landlord with dead eyes. "Consider the loss of your money a minor inconvenience," he said shortly.

"Freaks!" bellowed the landlord, realizing there was nothing he could do. He spun on his heels and pushed his way through the crowds toward Sneer Hall. "Dixon!" he shrieked. "I want you back on gate duty in two minutes—and NO POETRY!"

Luke helped his mom and dad to their feet. "Are you OK?" he asked.

Mrs. Watson nodded. "I suppose all I needed to help me change back was to hear your dad's voice."

Luke felt his cheeks burn. "I . . . I stopped him from coming to see you," he admitted.

"You did what you thought was best," said his dad, smiling fondly at him.

Resus came over and gave Luke a nudge. "Come on, wolf-boy," he said with a grin. "You don't want to miss the vampire family reunion!" Cleo joined the boys as they clambered out of the emporium and went to where Kian and his grandfather were standing.

"Tarlo Negative," declared Resus, holding up his palm to the elderly vampire, "I am Resus, of the glorious line of Negatov. I am honored to make your acquaintance."

"I presume you are offering me your palm, young vampire," said Tarlo. "It may be difficult for me to examine it, however." He gently tapped one of his cloudy, unseeing eyes.

"Oh," said Resus, reddening. "Sorry."

"I do not doubt your identity, Resus," Tarlo assured him. "For I sense that you carry something which once belonged to a common ancestor."

Resus searched under his cloak until he found the fang of Count Negatov, the first relic that he, Luke, and Cleo had found. "You can tell I've got this?" he asked in amazement.

He handed over the tooth and watched as the elderly vampire ran his fingers over its smooth surface.

"You would be surprised how my senses have improved since I lost my sight," said Tarlo.

Cleo smiled down at Kian, who was bouncing up and down excitedly, trying to get a glimpse of the relic. Then she sighed. "If only we could go back and choose not to take the fang in the first

place," she said, "we might not be surrounded by normals right now."

Luke grabbed her arm. "You're a genius!" he exclaimed.

"I am?" asked Cleo.

Resus laughed. "Don't tell me you're suggesting we go back in time!"

Luke shook his head impatiently and pulled *The G.H.O.U.L. Guide* from his pocket. "Mr. Skipstone!" he cried as the face on the cover opened its eyes. "I think I know how to close the doorway to Scream Street!"

"What?" demanded Cleo.

"How?" asked Resus.

Luke grinned at his friends. "Easy. We just have to give the six relics *back* to the founding fathers!"

TOMMY DONBAVAND

"Exactly the sort of grisly, gross, and hilarious stuff that kids will love!" —Eoin Colfer, author of *Artemis Fowl*

SCREAM STREET
FANG OF THE VAMPIRE

Free collectors' cards inside!

Meet Luke Watson: reluctant werewolf and Scream Street's latest arrival.

With his new friends Resus Negative (wannabe vampire) and Cleo Farr (tomboy mummy), Luke thinks Scream Street might just be somewhere he can call home. However, there's one small problem: his parents are terrified by their new neighbors. Can Luke find the doorway back to the real world before they're scared to death?

SCREAM STREET
Fangs for coming!

TOMMY DONBAVAND

"Exactly the sort of grisly, gross, and hilarious stuff that kids will love!" —Eoin Colfer, author of *Artemis Fowl*

SCREAM STREET
BLOOD OF THE WITCH

Free collectors' cards inside!

Scream Street has been invaded — by vampire rats. . . .

Luke, Resus, and Cleo are already on the trail of the second relic, a vial of witch's blood. But obstacles abound — first the evil Sir Otto Sneer turns off the blood supply, then a swarm of vampire rodents escapes, and now all the residents have been infected with vampire Energy! It looks as if Luke and his friends will have to choose between finding the relic and saving their neighbors. . . .

SCREAM STREET

Where blood is tastier than water!

"Exactly the sort of grisly, gross, and hilarious stuff that kids will love!" —Eoin Colfer, author of Artemis Fowl

TOMMY DONBAVAND

SCREAM STREET

HEART OF THE MUMMY

Free collectors' cards inside!

Scream Street just got darker. . . .

Scream Street has been shrouded in constant night for as long as anyone can remember, but things look really black when millions of spiders escape from No. 5, covering everything with their suffocating webs. Luke, Resus, and Cleo have their work cut out trying to combat the creepy-crawlies while searching for the third relic, the heart of the ancient mummy — and Sir Otto is determined to fight them every step of the way.

SCREAM STREET

It's no place like home!

The zombies have arrived
in Scream Street. . . .

Deadstock, the world's greatest zombie rock
festival, is here! Sir Otto Sneer, however, is not
in the mood for dancing — and causes a riot by
banishing headlining flesh-metal band Brain Drain
to the evil Underlands. If Luke and his friends
want to restore peace to the neighborhood and
find the relic they seek, they'll have to follow the
band . . . into the darkest depths of the earth.

SCREAM STREET

Dead pleased you dropped by!

There's a monster loose in Scream Street....

The legendary Headless Horseman has already
been causing a stir in the neighborhood, but when
the celebrity's head is stolen, there's an uproar!
Luke, Resus, and Cleo are swiftly on the case, but
Luke is on a headhunt of his own: to locate the
skull of Scream Street's first-ever skeleton. Sir Otto,
meanwhile, has created a monster to terrorize Luke
and force him to hand over the first four relics. It's
all he and his friends can do to keep their *own* heads!

SCREAM STREET

Bone-shakingly scary!

"Exactly the sort of grisly, gross, and hilarious stuff
that kids will love!" —Eoin Colfer, author of *Artemis Fowl*

TOMMY DONBAVAND

SCREAM STREET
CLAW OF THE WEREWOLF

Free collectors' cards inside!

Scream Street is full of surprises....

Luke is just one relic away from opening the gateway
back to his own world and finally taking his parents
from the terrors of Scream Street. And so begins the
hunt for the werewolf's claw. However, when he,
Resus, and Cleo discover an unexpected secret about
Samuel Skipstone, the author who has been invaluable
to their quest, they learn that the final relic comes
at a high cost. Faced with an impossible dilemma,
Luke is forced to make a very difficult decision.

SCREAM STREET

You'll roar for more!

Tommy Donbavand was born and raised in Liverpool, England, and has held a variety of jobs, including clown, actor, theater producer, children's entertainer, drama teacher, storyteller, and writer. His nonfiction books for children and their parents, *Boredom Busters* and *Quick Fixes for Bored Kids,* have helped him to become a regular guest on radio stations around the U.K. He also writes for a number of magazines, including *Creative Steps* and Scholastic's *Junior Education*.

Tommy sees the *Scream Street* series as what might have resulted had Stephen King been a writer for *Scooby-Doo.* "Writing the Scream Street books is fangtastic fun," he says. "I just have to be careful not to scare myself too much!" Tommy lives in England with his family and sees sleep as a waste of good writing time.

You can find out more about Tommy and his books at his website: www.tommydonbavand.com